EVADING

A REGENT VAMPIRE LORDS NOVEL #4

K.L. KREIG

E V A D I N G
Copyright © 2016 by K.L. Kreig

Published by K.L. Kreig
ISBN-13: 978-1-943443-11-6
ISBN-10: 1-943443-11-4

Cover Art by Yocla Designs
Editing by Nikki Busch Editing

Published in the United States of America.

To my Grandma Eleanor.

If you were still here, I'm not sure you would love my racy stories, but I know you would love my accomplishments. I feel your pride even from afar.

Thank you for your influence in shaping my life.

Author's Note:

This book certainly *can* be read as a standalone and still enjoyed. HOWEVER, this story does pick up in the middle of Mike and Giselle's relationship, to a degree. For their entire backstory to make sense, it's important to start with the three previous novels in the series, *Surrendering*, *Belonging*, and *Reawakening*

As this novel takes place during and shortly after *Reawakening*, for continuity purposes in storytelling, I have lifted a paragraph or two, or in one case, an exact partial scene as written in *Reawakening*. In addition, there are some minor threads created for future stories, but you will not have to read *Evading* to keep up, as I will reintroduce them in the next book.

This story is all about Mike and Giselle and how they finally find their way to each other and to their happily ever after.

Hang on. Grab some tissues. You're in for a bumpy ride. I hope you enjoy reading their story as much as I enjoyed writing it!

PROLOGUE

Giselle

Black death rained down around her. Each diabolical soul released for banishment into an eternal pit of flames and suffering was a breath of fresh air she could take once again. She relished each lungful.

Ancestry was destroyed.

Families decimated.

Retribution delivered.

She was the punisher.

She was deliverance.

She was hate.

She was vengeance.

Sweet, sweet vengeance.

Unrelenting pain—finally *theirs*—warmed her insides, lighting her ablaze.

Each filament attached to her limbs was a lethal weapon of inexorable suffering they couldn't escape. Saccharine lifeblood lifted to her nostrils. She took in the intoxicating, liberating scent.

Their bloodcurdling screams were music she wanted to savor for eternity.

Long sought after peace was finally within her grasp.

It hung like mist in the air around her, cooling her overheated flesh.

She felt it.

She tasted it.

It's all she thought about.

It's all she knew.

It's all she lived for.

It was finally hers and she would gladly serve her due penance for the devastation she'd just deluged.

CHAPTER 1

One Hundred Twenty years earlier...

Giselle

The sweet, fruity alcohol went down too well, too fast. It was her tenth, but it wasn't enough. There wasn't enough liquor in the world that could ease her suffering.

A slight tingle from the wine coursed through her bloodstream. That's all she'd get. Imbibing didn't do much for vampires, so she wasn't really sure why she bothered. But she needed something to keep her mouth, her hands, and her mind distracted so she wouldn't focus on events that had unfolded over the last day—events that would mean her own demise when Devon Fallinsworth, Midwest Regent Vampire Lord, caught up with her. And he would catch up with her...sooner rather than later, of that, she had no doubt.

That was okay, though. At least his justice would be swift. Merciful. Which was more than she'd been granted over the last five years. She'd accepted her fate. Looked forward to it, actually. Begged for it many a time over. Every time she was tied down. Every time she was violated. Every time those who were supposed to love her most broke her trust, using her body for their own selfish gain.

"This is your plight for what you are. Your penance. You took something from us and you will spend the rest of your days suffering for your pathetic existence."

The same words were repeated every time she was bound and blindfolded, naked, in that small, filthy room that smelled of wet dirt, mold, and perversion.

Human or vampire, it didn't matter. Bonded or single was irrelevant. Social status immaterial. They all were given a go, for the right price. Vampires were far rougher and liked to draw blood any way they could. Of course, many human males weren't that different. It's amazing how being completely at someone's mercy draws out the beast that hovers and lurks inside all of us, regardless of species.

Her brothers, the stupid twats, thought a paltry piece of fabric that took away her sight created anonymity for the males they let desecrate her day after day. But she knew every one of her abusers. Take away one of the senses and the others sharpen considerably.

Hers could cut glass.

She may not have seen them with her own eyes, but just like our DNA is unique, so, too, are our scents, the rhythm of our breaths, the ridges of flesh in our fingertips. The second they walked into that dank room and laid a hand on her, every characteristic was cataloged and tucked away.

And after five long years, it was done.

The righting of wrongs had been equaled.

All the intricate preparations had finally come to fruition. Every painful detail executed with near perfection.

The torment that started with her second blooding at fifteen ended with her final blooding yesterday at age twenty. She'd had one thousand eight hundred and twenty-five days to pour over every aspect of her vengeance.

She found flaws. Fixed them.

Practiced, reassessed.

Repetition, repetition, repetition. Until every scenario was covered, every defect eliminated. When you lived with the enemy, you got to know them pretty fucking well. Every chink, every weakness, every habit, no matter how small, could mean the difference between victory and failure.

They all thought she was weak, helpless, *hopeless.* But she wasn't. She was just fucking smarter than they were, biding her time until she could unleash the beast they'd created.

Giselle had been victorious, cutting down each offender with stealth and efficiency and no fucking mercy, starting with her two brothers. Every one of them was now rotting in a hell of their own making.

Except one.

Somehow, he'd known she was coming for him and had fled. She'd spent the last twenty-four hours hunting him so she could go to her grave with a clear conscience and no regrets, but he remained elusive.

And didn't that figure? He was the most sadistic, evil bastard of them all. A weekly regular since day one, he delivered punishing blows and vicious agony. But he never left any visible marks behind. Instead, he left the worst kind of scars that never healed. And since he was vampire, he had countless days yet to deliver his special brand of pain to other innocents.

The worst of it was he was also her pappi's best friend. He was supposed to love her like a daughter, not treat her like a whore. Like her brothers, he preached about "leading by example," only no one ever suspected he was a vile, malevolent creature who preferred the screams and cries of an innocent to that of his own mate.

As long as she remained free, she'd track him. She'd find him. Then she'd end him, too. Only then, would she rest. She may go to hell for the retribution she'd unleashed, but she was not about to go down without dragging the bloody remains of every last one of those sick fucks that preyed on the young and weak. She'd drop them personally at Lucifer's feet with a smile on her face and consummation pumping in her veins.

She threw back the cool wine, signaling for another when she felt *them*.

"Giselle Petrova?"

Her heart sank to her feet. *Shit*. Time was up.

The thought of fleeing briefly crossed her mind, but only so she could end what she'd started, not to escape punishment. Even if she did make an attempt, in her heart she knew she wouldn't get far. Lord Devon wouldn't send just any lunks to bring in a mass murderer. He'd send his best.

No. This was the end of the line for her. She sealed her fate with the first strike of her sword. And payment would be in the form of her own life. She'd been prepared for this outcome from the very beginning. At least, it would be on *her* terms, under her control. And she'd hold her head high until her last breath, proud that she'd rid the world of at least a few slivers of evil.

Breathing deeply, she stood, squaring her shoulders. "Yes."

"Lord Devon has required your presence. Come with us."

Her gaze swam over the two broad, handsome vampires who were clearly old and powerful. Definitely, more of a match than she could take. Standing, she allowed lefty to grab her elbow, and while his grip was firm, it wasn't bruising.

Once outside, in the safety of the grove and away from humans, they flashed to a modern-day dungeon of sorts: packed dirt floors, crumbling stone walls, and cells with thick, wrought iron bars. Not much different than the way she'd lived.

They placed her in a dank, musty unit and closed the door, their faces remaining impassive. She was sure they used the same magic her brothers had to imprison her. A halfhearted attempt to escape proved that theory out.

This is was it, then—the end of a long, desolate road. In just a matter of hours, her existence would be no more. All that would remain of her were glorified stories of a heinous act no one would ever fully understand. She waited for sadness to drown her, but it never came. Instead, she felt a strange, calming peace settle in her bones.

Sliding down to the floor, Giselle leaned back against the cool rock and released a genuine sigh of relief. Yes, she was imprisoned and death loomed, yet she was actually smiling. Relishing in the fact she was *free*.

Tonight would be the first night in over five years she wouldn't be raped and tortured. She wouldn't be bound. She wouldn't be in pain. She wouldn't be belittled or bled or scourged. Her stomach wouldn't cramp with hunger. She would actually be able to open her eyes and see something other than the color black.

She was free. Blessedly, truly free.

She wanted to bask in her newfound independence for every minute she had left, but the lethargy she'd been fighting began to win. The adrenaline, which had pumped her up over the last twenty-four hours took a nosedive, sending her crashing. Unable to keep her eyes open, she gave in to its pull.

This time, though, instead of the usual nightmares that plagued her, she dreamed of her mammi: a female Giselle had never known because she'd died while giving birth to her. Giselle's lifetime of torment at the hand of her brothers was her punishment for taking both her parents' lives. And for being female, she thought. Would a male have suffered her same fate? She didn't think so.

The dream started out with Giselle as a little girl. She sat on a shaky, three-legged wooden stool, balanced on

K . L . K R E I G

an uneven earth floor as her mammi stood behind brushing her blonde locks in languid, easy strokes, singing an unfamiliar tune. Her mammi stood for hours in that exact same spot, singing the exact same song, grooming her the exact same way. She brushed so long Giselle's head started to hurt, but she begged her not to stop because each pull of the coarse brush was mystical, turning the strands into spun gold.

"Mammi, what's happening?" she asked, staring in awe at the heavy gild in her tiny hand.

"It's magic, my darling. But it can only happen to those who are noble and pure."

But that was wrong. Giselle wasn't noble and pure; she was vile and hated. She didn't know how she knew that...she just did.

"No, Mammi. You're wrong. I'm not noble or pure."

Her beautiful mammi leaned down to whisper, "Mammis are never wrong about what matters most, Giselle. I'm sorry I left." Drops of disgrace chased down her face, one after the other, falling into a pool of water that rapidly swelled around her. Panicking, she looked back to her mammi for help, but she was gone. When Giselle glanced down again, the water now lapping at her waist wasn't really water at all.

It was thick and scarlet and held the sins of men. It rose quick, like a tide, and threatened to drown her where she'd be eternally trapped in their unanswered, undeserving pleas for mercy.

Just as she was going under, the scene morphed. Now she stared at a vision of herself covered in blood and hate and violence. A gore-covered sword hung limply in her hand. Once-shiny gold locks were now caked with dirt and relief. Taking in the carnage all around her, her heart was equally dense and weightless.

Her mammi's disembodied voice whispered, "You've made me proud."

"But I killed your sons," she replied on a sob.

"You righted wrongs, Giselle. There is honor in that."

The cackle of unrepentant evil in the distance taunted her. "One got away."

"Karma chases the perverse, though sometimes she needs an edge."

The rattling of the cell door woke her. Giselle jumped to her feet in defense, momentarily forgetting where she was. The vivid dream hung over her like a thick fog she couldn't shake.

"Female, it's time," the handsome vampire chimed.

Blinking off the last remnants of the illusion, she simply nodded. Resigned to her fate, Giselle followed without a fight. Eyes forward, back straight. As they wound down hallways, marching toward her penance, though, she couldn't stop hearing her mammi's words.

"Karma chases the perverse, though sometimes she needs an edge."

A flash of remorse fired hotly through her, but it wasn't because of the lives she'd taken. It was because of the one she hadn't.

Giselle had originally vowed to go to her grave silent. In her mind's eye, she was justified in every casualty that sullied her hands, and she would not repent or defend or explain. No one deserved a fucking thing from her.

But what if Lord Devon was karma's edge? What if he believed her story? What if *he* was the conduit to vet due justice since she wouldn't be able to?

If she said nothing—*did* nothing—she would never know and Siobhan would win.

He couldn't win. He couldn't *live*. He didn't deserve to take another breath while she was punished for righting evil wrongs. If she didn't stop him or at least try, the realization that she'd failed would haunt her for all eternity. She couldn't live with that.

She had to do this one last thing. As abhorrent as the thought was.

Mind made up, in her final words she'd humble and humiliate herself, revealing repulsions no one should ever hear. Relive degradation she could barely acknowledge had happened to *her*.

In her last breaths, Giselle would remain strong. She'd do it in hopes that the Midwest Regent Vampire Lord was as benevolent and fair as everyone said he was. And that he'd exact the justice she needed so she could finally rest in a peace she had more than earned.

CHAPTER 2

Present

Giselle

White-hot fire bathed her back, her arms, her thighs. Each blow rained fresh hell on her anew, peeling the tender skin from her body until warm, sticky blood pooled beneath her kneeled form.

In debilitating agony, her eyes fell to the ground, the hallucination clawing at her until her mind was also raw.

No pool of warmth bathed her flesh.

No gore lined the hard surface underneath her knees.

Yet the pain remained.

Real. Pure. Unbearable.

She was helpless once again. Something she swore she would never be.

"Ah, I can see you're confused, ma chérie," that dark, repugnant voice crooned. It was him. Siobhan. The one who had escaped his punishment so long ago. Or was that just yesterday?

"*Non. Not Siobhan, mon amour.*" Something ran along her cheek, the tenderness of the act belying the sadistically malevolent tone. "*Who am I, you ask? I'm everyone and no one. I'm the Messiah and the Dark One. I'm eternal light and everlasting blackness. And I'll breathe the very life back into your worst fucking nightmares, Giselle.*" Her drawn-out name sounded like poison on his spiked tongue, the ends piercing her flesh like a thousand needles. "*You can't run. You can't hide. You can only endure. Now...let's start again, shall we?*"

This the time the pain centered in the very core of her being, a place she'd never let anyone willingly enter. She was being torn in two, but her physical flesh, nerves, muscles, and bones didn't matter. They would heal. They would heal so they could be violated over and again. No...it was her soul that would be shredded beyond all recognition. It was her soul that would die black and shriveled and hollow.

She began to pray for darkness that would never come.

———————

Giselle jolted from her nightmare drenched in a cold sweat, breathing ragged, heart racing. Phantom pain lingered on her flesh. Her screams still echoed in her ears. Her mind was cloudy, making her weak, vulnerable. Defenseless.

It's not real. It's not happening. You're not there.

It was a dream. A horrible, hellish, insufferable dream.

You are fine.

You are fine.

Just fine.

Breathing deeply and slowly, Giselle willed her heart rate to slow. She'd let her guard down, something she never did, and she struggled to remember why. Why did she feel safe enough to let sleep take her under so hard?

She tried to move, but steely arms banded tightly, holding her still. Fear should have her on the defensive, but instinctively, she knew she was safe. Safer than she'd ever been. It was a foreign feeling her sleep-fogged brain still struggled to reconcile.

Before she could get her bearings, a baritone timbre rumbled sleepily in her ear, "Shhh, baby. I got you."

That voice. She recognized that deep, sexy voice. It was balm that soothed her scarred soul. It was the male she'd tried for the past year to forget. To ignore. To hate. To leave behind.

The same male who'd told her earlier tonight he loved her.

Loved. Her.

Her.

Giselle Petrova.

She still fought to wrap her head around it. How could Mike Thatcher possibly love her when he didn't even know her? Not really. Didn't he understand she was ruined, broken, scarred, stained, repulsive, coldhearted? Whatever word that best described the unlovable?

That was her. Unlovable.

She shouldn't be here, leading him on. She should have left his ass the minute he said it and never looked back. No...what she should have done was twisted his balls until they snapped off and *then* left his ass and never looked back.

But she didn't. She stayed. She willingly allowed him to carry her back to his bed, lay her down next to him, and hold her close. She remained silent when he stripped her down to her panties and kissed her hair. She lay perfectly still while he stroked her back and whispered sweet fucking nothings in her ear. She let herself be lulled into thinking this, this...*thing*...between them was a real possibility, when it wasn't.

But did she leave? Even then?

Fuck no.

Here it was. Hours later. The middle of the night and here she still lay. In his house. Between his sheets. Wrapped in his arms. Everything inside her was speed melting underneath his warmth and affection when she needed to stay frozen, unaffected, and unattached instead. Unfortunately, around Mike Thatcher, it was becoming more arduous and precarious to accomplish.

He'd changed her in ways she didn't like. In fact, she hated them. He made her soft. He made her care. The gorgeous asshole made her *feel*, goddammit. And removing the frigid barriers she'd erected caused old emotions to boil hot and closer to the surface than she was comfortable with. She could practically see the ashy singe on her skin from memories of ancient horrors.

Nothing good could come of what they were doing.

Nothing.

Both of them would get hurt.

Then why am I still here?

"Uh, uh. You're not running, beautiful." Mike tightened his hold as she tried to rise again, his tone now hard, unyielding, his grip bordering on pain.

She huffed and relaxed back into him, fully intent on leaving whenever the fuck she wanted. The fact she didn't *really* want to leave pissed her off even more. She'd let this human burrow himself under her skin further than the teeth of a bur. A place she'd only allowed two others in her entire life to go, and it took them decades to break through the concrete her flesh had become. The detective had managed the same task in mere months.

"You do realize you can't keep me here, asshole. Right?"

She was being a royal bitch when he'd been nothing

but kind to her the last few days, but she couldn't help it. Sarcasm was instinct. Giselle tried hard not remember how it had easily taken a back seat to the fun they'd been having. *Yes, fun.* They'd laughed, talked, traded light barbs, and worked in easy tandem as if they'd been doing it for years. He'd let her *feed* from him for Christ's sake and he would never understand what it took for her to do that. And now that she had, how hard it was for her not to do it again. The scent of his blood howled her name. It belonged to her.

This time, though, would be for sheer indulgence versus voracious need. And *that*, more than just about anything, scared the hell out of her. She'd never once taken blood for pleasure. Not once.

Mike turned her toward him, framing her face with his large, manly human hands. They were calloused and thick and they felt so damn good on her icy skin, every touch evaporating that frigidness just a tiny bit more.

Damn him.

She needed to go.

She wanted to stay.

"Yeah, I realize you can pull your Houdini act and be gone in a flash, pun intended. But I want you to stay. I'm *asking* you to stay, Giselle."

The need she heard, as though she was essential to his very being, halted her snide retort. They had camaraderie. They'd both been living life in the dark. In pain. Buried alive. Each breath full of toxic memories they wished would mercifully kill them, but hatefully wouldn't.

Why was he the only male in her one hundred forty-one years who'd been able to lighten her baggage? Counteract the poison?

You know exactly why, Giselle. You just won't acknowledge it.

"Please," he urged, holding her stare. That was a

word he used sparingly. Mike Thatcher didn't beg for a damn thing. He took what he wanted and made no apologies for it. Ever. If he were any other way, she wouldn't be tangled in his bed right now. She shouldn't be anyway.

Holding her eyes, he lowered his head until his lips touched hers, tentatively, at first, seeking permission. They pressed harder, taking more, demanding it all. She gave it. Gave in. Gave out, whatever. She was weak. So very fucking weak when it came to him. His touch scrambled her brains, knocked into her barricades like an unrelenting battering ram. Shit was flying loose everywhere.

"Stay," he demanded gruffly between light bites.

Mike's intense want thundered through her body like a jet engine, fueling her own desire. While that feeling emanating from a male would have repulsed her in the past, she now found herself wondering what type of lover the detective would be if she could only allow herself to say yes. Gentle and loving? Rough and demanding? The perfect combination of dirty and sweet? The temptation to find out had grown to an almost unquenchable thirst she needed to assuage.

But she didn't know how. She'd never done any of this before with a male.

Giselle's sultry persona was just that. A guise, a front, a role she played. She was full of show and cocky declarations—and utter *bullshit*—because the truth was she hadn't been intimate with a male since the day before her last blooding at age twenty. She'd never had free will growing up and, from the time Dev granted her amnesty she'd exercised her choice to abstain.

She'd never swayed on that decision until the obstinate detective came along, tempting her beyond all reason, popping her celibacy lock. He was the golden ticket. The key. She craved him on a weird, uncomfortable level she couldn't ignore anymore.

Giselle had allowed Mike Thatcher to explore places on her that were pure and untouched, at least in the way he was doing it. She'd never been worshipped or given pleasure that was solely for her. Every graze of his fingers or nip of his dull teeth awakened her more, pulling womanly desires from the deep bogs within. She never knew it could be this way between a male and a female.

"Stay," he cajoled again, convincingly dragging his tongue along the swell of her breasts before dipping further to suck a painfully peaked nipple. When one hand gently fisted her hair while the other tunneled down the back of her panties, she mentally caved. Her soul was starved for affection, her body weeping to be adored.

"Touch me." *Make me forget* is really what she meant.

Drawing his hand around from her ass to the wet space between her thighs, she silently begged. He pulled back to make sure it was okay. He always did that, and as always, the sweet gesture made her fall into him, getting herself lost once again. And, as always, her answer was to slant her mouth over his, telling him with her body everything she couldn't with words.

Once again, she let him stroke her, drive her up, take her over. She writhed in sweet pleasure underneath his magical fingers as they demanded she go places she'd never wanted to go before. Now, she couldn't get enough of it. When he'd wrung everything she could give, her body just as sated as if she'd fed, he settled his front to her back and told her to sleep, not expecting anything in return. Even though his stiff, throbbing desire prodded between her cheeks, he made no move to take care of it or ask her to.

Just another thing about him to like. His selflessness.

God, this all felt good. *Too* good. Every last bit of it.

But what happened if he found out about her? About

the blood on her hands and the wounds on her spirit? About the smears of sin that still felt smothering and base? What would he think of her then? How could he love her then?

Mother of all fucks.

Her head now buzzed for an entirely different reason. Giselle tried to relax. Tried shutting herself down, tried enjoying the warmth still deliciously humming through her veins, but a whirlwind of thoughts raced at warp speed, easily sweeping all the good away until all that remained were doubts.

What the fuck are you doing, Elle?

Blood just because?

Touch for pleasure?

Cuddling? Cud-dul-ing?

No. That wasn't her.

That could *never* be her.

Could it?

No. No, it couldn't. Jesus, she'd made the gravest of mistakes. She had her head so far in the goddamned clouds she was seeing promises that didn't exist. Wanting a future she couldn't have. Wanting a whole host of shit she didn't want to want, but couldn't stop wanting anyway.

Giselle was ruined. Tainted. Untold DNA stained her skin, her soul, her body both inside and out. She wasn't fit to befriend someone, let alone be much, much more than that to this incredible male holding her.

Her icy exterior was turning slushy, and that was unacceptable. Hell, he'd worn down her sharp edges so much already she was actually here because she was doing Rom's mate a favor. A *favor*, for the love of Christ. Giselle did *not* do favors. The foreign word tasted bitter on her tongue. She wanted to spit it out and grind it into the ground with a spiked heel.

She should have never allowed them to go this far. She'd made a huge mistake spending so much time with

Mike, dropping her guard, letting him too close. She needed space to think, to breathe, to reevaluate.

Feeling clammy and panicky, she willed herself to the place of inner frozen calm she expertly tapped into until his breaths gradually softened to a slow, even cadence.

Then, when she knew he was fast asleep, she stealthily slipped out of bed and dressed. With one last longing glance she once again left her Fated behind, all the while lying to herself she was doing it to protect him from her when it was so obviously the other way around.

CHAPTER 3

Mike

He'd woken this morning and Giselle was gone. Classic. Totally expected, yet, soul crushing nonetheless. But surprisingly...he wasn't mad at her. He was mad at himself. He *knew* he was moving too fast. He knew she might not be in the same place he was emotionally. Hell, she may *never* be. Maybe he was just a shiny new plaything to her and nothing more. But even as he thought it, he knew it wasn't true. The feelings she had for him could not be hidden in her expressive eyes. She just couldn't verbalize them. Therefore, he should have kept his big fucking mouth shut and maybe she'd still be here right now.

He got her message loud and clear. She apparently needed space, so he'd give it to her.

"To what do I owe the pleasure of your summoning, human?"

"You're such a fucking prick, bloodsucker," Mike muttered under his breath before stepping aside to let Renaldo enter his humble abode.

Fuck if he wanted him here, but fuck if he had any choice either. He may have decided not to contact Giselle directly when he woke to a cold and empty bed after begging her to stay in the middle of the night, but he never said he wouldn't find out what the hell was going on with the woman he was in love with either.

The only way he knew how to do that was through Devon's powerful lieutenant. By the way, Renaldo threatened to, let's see, *personally cut out his shriveled-up heart after he first sucked his body dry of every single drop of blood,* several months back if he hurt Giselle, he had an inkling they were pretty close.

Which didn't sit too well with him, by the way.

In fact, it didn't fucking sit well at all.

"You know, along with superpowers, cat-like agility, and sound-of-light speed, us bloodsuckers have a very keen sense of hearing. Prick," Ren declared without venom as he swaggered on by.

Mike couldn't help it. He laughed. "Touché."

"Where's Giselle?"

"I was going to ask you the same. Beer?" he offered on his way to the fridge. He was never one to care about so-called rules when it came to imbibing. If he wanted a beer with breakfast, he'd have a fucking beer with breakfast.

"What the hell. Sure."

Mike took two Bud heavies and popped the tops before handing a cold brew to the tall, broad vampire now leaning against his faded yellow kitchen wall. He didn't like the way Ren was already scrutinizing him. Had he any self-preservation left in his weary body, he would be intimidated by his enormous size and bulk and perceptive stare. Alas, he'd lost that care years ago.

Except now...now he wondered if that still held true. If Giselle wanted him, he definitely had something to live for. And that's what he aimed to find out right now.

"I know you didn't ask me here to shoot the shit and play beer pong, so why the hell am I standing in your cracker box kitchen when I have better things to do?"

"So you haven't talked to Giselle, then?" he asked, trying to sound nonchalant instead of agitated.

"Why?"

Mike shrugged. "You two seem pretty tight."

Ren regarded him for a few solid heartbeats. "Contrary to your beliefs, Detective, I am not her fucking secretary or her keeper. Giselle does what she wants when she wants. The only one she listens to is Dev," the too-arrogant-for-his-pants vamp replied smoothly.

"Don't I fucking know it," Mike mumbled in agreement.

Ren took a healthy swallow from his bottle before asking, "What'd you do to piss her off?"

This was it. Do or die time. Should he confide his feelings about Giselle to Lord Devon's second in command? If he did, would he end up watching his heart pulse its last few beats in Ren's hand before he took his final dirt nap?

Turns out he didn't need to say a word.

"Oh fuck. I know that look." Ren started shaking his head. His face was impassive and that pissed Mike the hell off.

"What look?" he barked defensively.

"The 'hopelessly devoted to you' look, asshole. You went and fell in love with her, didn't you?" Ren generally showed no emotion, unless it was impudence, but his tone bordered on challenge.

He didn't know the nature of the relationship between Giselle and Ren, but he'd always secretly worried that Ren had more than "friendly" feelings toward *his* woman or they had some sort of past. Even though Ren had tried pushing them together not that long ago, he wouldn't put anything past the blood drinker. Push Mike toward Giselle and then bury him six feet under for touching her sounded like just the justification the bloodsucker needed to slit his throat without ramifications.

Well, fuck that shit. Giselle belonged to *him*.

Mike straightened to his full height. At six foot two,

he was a fairly tall guy but was still several inches shorter than Ren's impressive six-six stature. Standing toe-to-toe with a species that could gut him and bury him faster than he could sing "The Star-Spangled Banner" was not a smart move on anyone's part, but especially his. It was no secret that Detective Mike Thatcher wasn't a fan favorite of the plasma drinkers or vice versa. But fuck all if he cared. Giselle was his. *His.*

"Why? Do I have competition?"

He hated the fact he had to look up to this fucker as heavy silence thickened between the two. Insinuations, anger, and power shimmered in the air, nearly taking solid form. Then a broad grin formed on Ren's lips and it stretched until the cocksucker was laughing. Hard and loud.

"What the hell is so funny, bloodsucker?" Mike spat.

That made Ren's chortle pick up until he was nearly doubled over with some fucking joke that apparently only he could hear. Regret ate at his gut—why had he thought this was a good idea in the first place?

"Does she know how you feel?" the vamp finally asked when he'd gotten control of himself, taking an uninvited seat at the worn dining table like he planned to stick around for some lighthearted chitchat. The chair creaked when he let his large bulk relax into the rickety wood.

Trying to remain stoic, Mike didn't answer, but rage still pulsed madly through him. The irritating sound of fingers drumming filled the silence. He wanted to cut those fingers off and feed them to his next-door neighbor's dog, Fluff. Don't be fooled by the name. Fluff was a rabid pit bull who would sooner tear into your calf muscle than scare you away with his equally vicious bark. His neighbor had a very sick sense of humor.

Ren was either a mind-fucking-reader or Mike was bad at hiding his emotions because Ren's lips turned down before he said what could well be taken as sincere sympathy. "Well, there you go, human. That's why you can't find her."

He didn't want to ask. He didn't want to continue this conversation at all, but the question was out before he could shove it back in. "What exactly does that mean?"

Ren nodded to the empty chair across from him. Mike only moved when the asshole raised one cocky brow that clearly said: *If you're getting any information from me, you'll sit your ass down.*

Reluctantly, he slid into the seat, every muscle on red alert, and waited for the vamp who seemed to know Giselle better than anyone to respond. Jealousy burned him at that thought.

"You know I don't really like you, right?" Ren said coolly.

"Good thing I don't give a flying rat's asshole what you like, vampire."

Ignoring his insult, the jackass continued. "But Giselle does. And even I'm not daft enough that I can't admit you're good for her, so I'm going to let you in on a little four-one-one about our seductress, Detective. But if you tell her it came from me, I'll deny it before I gut you."

Taking a chance, Mike replied snarkily, "She'd kill you if you laid a hand on me."

A cocky smirk curled the vamp's lips. "She would try, which is the only reason I'm gifting you with this tidbit of intelligence."

"I'm listening."

Ren leaned forward on the table, crossing his bulky arms in front of him. He dropped his voice low as if there were others in the room who may overhear. "Giselle is more fragile than she appears to be."

Mike waited for him to continue. To give him some *new* information on the female he was pining after like a damn lovesick fool, but the bloodsucker remained quiet, silently studying him for a reaction.

"That's it? That's your fucking revelation? That she's wounded like we all are?" He leaned forward toward the vampire, mirroring his position. "Newsflash, asshole. I saw through her cocky bravado months ago."

"Good."

"Good."

The smug bastard leaned back and finished his cocktail. "Beer me."

"You're fucking kidding me, right? There's a convenience store down the road on your way out." He nodded to his front door, giving the vamp a hint.

Ren chuckled and stood. Placing his massive mitts on the table, he hovered over Mike. The laminate creaked under his two hundred thirty-plus pounds of solid muscle. Mike didn't lean back, even a fraction. "She's running scared, but that means you're getting to her. Getting close. Under her skin. In her head. And I have to tell you, human, no one gets to Elle. She gets to them."

"Tell me something I don't already know."

"Don't give up."

"The fires of hell wouldn't stop me," he replied adamantly.

Nodding sharply, the vampire made his way toward the exit. Mike stayed seated, disgustedly marveling at how a large creature could move with such stealth and grace.

With the knob in his hand, Ren turned back. "Your future with her rests squarely on your shoulders, I'm afraid to say. Giselle never takes the easy road and it's hard for her to accept what's staring her in the goddamned face, so don't blink. Don't look away. Don't give her a fucking inch or she'll be gone. But most importantly, Detective, make her feel safe." After a slight pause, he clarified, "To be clear, what I'm saying is *emotionally* safe. She's been through more than your puny little human mind can possibly comprehend."

Mike wanted to throw a punch in that smug bastard's face and Ren knew it. But he wanted information more.

"What happened to her when she was taken by that sadistic bastard, Ren?" He hated to ask but needed to know. She'd been frosty cold before, but after her kidnapping by Xavier, she'd been different. Fragile. Like she'd turned to dry ice and one wrong touch would set a series of cracks and fissures into slow motion that he wouldn't be able to stop. He was terrified he'd be forced to watch her helplessly shatter into pieces right before his eyes, her fragments scattered at his feet.

That's part of the reason he asked the vampire here today. Giselle would never tell him. She was a damn vault, but he was working on breaking the lock. Bit by agonizing bit. If he could just get a little help, it would be so much easier.

Ren's face sobered. "You know as much as I do."

"I don't know shit."

"Exactly."

He nodded, surprised Ren didn't know and disappointed he was unable to learn anything new, except for possibly the depth that Giselle bled. *Huh*...guess he knew more about his woman than he gave himself credit for.

Mike was temporarily lost in his own thoughts when Ren added, "You weren't really trying to take me on, were you?"

"And if I was?" He raised a mocking brow.

"Well, you are either the stupidest fucker I've met or the ballsiest. And if you're going to pursue Elle, you'd better have balls forged of titanium and the patience of Job, my friend. You're gonna need 'em both."

"Already covered." Ren was halfway out when Mike called, "One more thing, vampire. She's not *your* seductress. She's mine."

With his index finger, Ren touched his temple and

then pointed at Mike, a smirk on his face. "Touché."

He could have sworn he saw a hint of respect in the powerful vampire's eyes before he disappeared, leaving Mike to wonder if he was reading between the lines correctly. Was the overprotective Renaldo actually *encouraging* him to chase—and, more importantly, *catch*—Giselle? If he was, what exactly did that mean?

Deciding he wasn't going to solve world hunger today or ever unravel the inner workings of a vampire's complex mind, he went back to work on the pet project Giselle had asked for his help with—tracking down Sarah Hill's lineage.

Buckling down, he contacted additional PDs and faxed pictures of the two missing women. He'd worked tirelessly for hours, all the while trying to forget how they sat on the couch next to each other and watched *The Late Show* or how she let him take her hand when they took a walk at dusk last night or how he taught her the finer art of making frozen fish sticks. He wasn't successful blocking her from his thick head, but about an hour ago...he did hit pay dirt.

Marna Clark was age twenty when she went missing in Des Plains, Illinois in 1969. There were very few leads and her case quickly grew cold and was eventually forgotten in favor of the newest missing person. Hundreds of thousands of people go missing each year in the United States alone, and Marna quickly became a statistic, like so many others. Mike was able to get her parents' names, number, and address. He'd called but there was no answer.

Fuck it. Des Plains was only an hour and fifteen minutes from Milwaukee and since there was no reason to stick around here, he grabbed his phone, packed an overnight bag, and headed to the garage. He'd sleep in a cheap motel close to their house and stop by the Clarks' first thing in the morning. Talking to them in person would be better anyway. He could gauge their expressions and, more importantly, see their faces. Did either of them resemble Sarah? Did they have other children who did?

He didn't really understand why Giselle was working on this project for Sarah since Giselle wasn't really the warm and fuzzy type, but the reason didn't matter. Even if she'd decided not to come back, he would continue on his own. He'd do it for Sarah. He'd do it to keep his goddamned mind from spinning and churning.

And he'd do it in hopes that Giselle would come to her fucking senses and return to him. This time for good. Because next time she walked through that door, he wasn't letting her leave. Ever.

CHAPTER 4

Giselle

Sitting in the kitchen, alone in the dark, Giselle took a long drink of her vodka and pondered the events of the last several months.

Of the interminable war with Xavier.

Of her torture at his minions' hands.

Of the unusual fact all three Regent Vampire Lords had met and bonded with their Moiras within the last six months.

But mostly, she thought about one Detective Mike Thatcher.

She knew the moment their eyes met almost a year ago now that he was hers. He was her Fated. The only male meant for her.

But she hadn't been looking for her mate. She didn't *want* to be tied to any male. *Ever*. She'd been perfectly content alone.

Until *he* showed up.

And changed everything.

He'd fucking changed *everything*.

And try as she might to fight it—*them*—she was failing. Horribly.

She'd never seen a male—human or vampire—as beautiful as Mike. He was built and bulky for a human. Sensual need always swirled in his stormy blue, hooded eyes, which were framed by thick, dark lashes and brows. The scruff he wore well gave him a rough-hewn sort of vibe that fit him perfectly.

But his mouth—that's what really got her. His lips cut through bullshit and his tongue was razor sharp. His barbs and verbal sparring went straight to her sex, making her hot and needy.

He was her match. Her equal.

Not one person she'd ever run across had gotten to her like the detective. Every single time she saw him, he'd pluck another thorn from her prickly persona, leaving the tiniest of holes that she couldn't cover quick enough before he wormed his way underneath. That left her vulnerable. Shaken to her fucking core. And pissed off as hell. She needed those damn thorns. They were the only things protecting her fragile insides. Her skin was a rose bed of them...and the bed was thinning quickly.

Not knowing how to deal, she did something she was not proud of. Going against the grain that made her who she was.

She *ran*.

From him.

From herself.

From *them*.

In the beginning, it was self-preservation. The detective detested her kind and in some twisted way she understood. Xavier had taken away the female he thought he was supposed to spend his life with. But he wasn't meant to spend it with Jamie. He was meant to spend it with *her*; he just didn't know it. And he certainly would never accept it. Didn't that just figure. He hated her guts because of something that was completely out of her control.

Same story. New century. Different male.

Try as she might, though, she couldn't seem to escape him. They'd been incessantly thrown together now for months on end and it was a daily struggle to keep her feelings hidden. They both pushed each other's buttons. Danced around their feelings. It felt an awful lot like a game of cat and mouse. While Giselle was *always* the stealthy feline, in this particular game she was most definitely the timid prey. Goading him was all fun and games until she realized he actually wanted her back.

But now...now she ran because...well, she was scared. Terrified, really. Humans and vampires were no different when it came to the ugly truth. They would say they want to know you, the *real* you, but once you let them inside, they'd want to turn away because viewing genuine ugliness through a clear lens is like getting a sneak peek into hell. It's impossible to comprehend the depths of deviance and depravity others are capable of, and seeing it up close and personal means you can't deny it's real anymore.

And when you loved someone, you opened that fucking door and let all your insides pour out. The good, the bad, and the *ugly*.

So this...

"I love you, Giselle."

...this was almost too much to handle.

He'd want to see her ugly and she couldn't let him.

So where did that leave them?

She really didn't know.

It had been more than twenty-four hours since she'd left without a word, running scared. Twenty-four hours during which she'd done nothing but think about him and replay his confession over and over again..."*I love you, Giselle.*" And while it made her sick at how those simple words sent flutters through her belly, she could finally admit that she loved him back. Hell, since the moment she'd laid eyes on him, she was in love with his smart mouth and sexy-as-sin ass. But knowing it and admitting it out loud, especially to him, were two totally different things.

She loved him but she didn't deserve him, and she didn't know what to do about it. Soul-searching hadn't helped. That ended up being a vicious cycle of acceptance, then confusion, then anger. She was getting dizzy trying to deny what they were but wanting it all the same. Convincing herself why it may work, then justifying her spineless decision to cut out on him.

Still, without answers, all she knew was she missed him terribly and desperately needed to see him again. But when she finally drummed up the courage to face him, the bastard was nowhere to be found.

She hadn't heard from him since she'd slunk out like the coward she was. He didn't call. He hadn't texted. He'd been radio silent. At first, she couldn't quite decide if that thrilled her or angered her. But as the hours passed, it was pretty clear which emotion she was feeding from.

Her slow burn had turned into a raging boil.

So here she sat, stalking Mike fucking Thatcher like a goddamned idiot. And by stalking, what she really meant was crazy-ass, balls-to-the-wall, nonstop hounding. If she were human, she'd probably be in jail by now. Phone calls, text messages, pacing the length of his porch waiting for his home to show any signs of life. But he was just gone, so in addition to getting worried, she was now a volcano of ugly pissiness ready to blow.

He'd begged her to stay. Demanded it, actually. Fingered her until she melted under him. Why, then, was he now avoiding her? Maybe the endorphins from the orgasm they'd both pumped him to while she drank down his lifeblood loosened his tongue and lips and he hadn't meant what he'd said. Maybe he realized he'd been wasting his time. That she wasn't worth it. That she was too damaged to invest any more effort into.

Maybe he was finally done with her. That thought sat hard and hated in the pit of her stomach.

Hearing a noise, she looked up to find Ren padding into the darkened room.

"Hey, baby girl," he greeted, pulling a bowl of fruit out of the fridge.

Dev's security detail, which included Ren, Manny, Thane, and herself, lived at the mansion with Dev. Manny and Thane were close and shared the same wing of the house, but both Ren and Giselle had their own private quarters. Over the years, she'd become used to living with "roommates." Most of the time, it was convenient. Except when it wasn't. Like now.

Taking another drink, she relished the slow burn all the way to her stomach. "Why do you insist on calling me that?" she growled, needing to take her anger out on someone. Besides Ren, she would sooner cut out someone's tongue before allowing them to use an endearment with her.

Except Mike. I let him call me baby all the time.
Shut up dammit!

"Because it riles you up." The smooth smile that lit his face was brilliant. Ren was one of the best-looking males she had ever met, but she'd never been attracted to him as a female should. He was more like the brother she should have had. Ren and Dev, *they* were her family. Had been ever since Dev saved her.

"You feed recently?" Ren asked.

Yet another secret of hers that Ren held tight to.

Using Mike the way she had was something she hadn't done since the day she was fully blooded.

In dire situations, vampires fed from bagged blood, but that was like tofu. It was empty, unsatisfying, barely nutritional. Vampires really needed a live host to thrive. Males fed from female humans and female vamps fed from male humans. It was the way for them. Except her. Giselle couldn't stomach the thought of touching a male in that way because that would lead to sex, so she'd either nourish herself from a willing female at one of Dev's clubs or use the bagged crap.

Her belly constricted now just thinking of Mike's taste—having it on her tongue and running through her veins again. It was Eden. God, her mouth watered.

"I'm good." Her voice sounded thready, wobbly. He smirked and she ignored him, taking another sip.

"Why aren't you with your detective now?"

Her retort was hot and fast. "He's not mine."

"Yeah, he is," he taunted knowingly. "Have you fucked him yet?"

No, but God how I want to. "Jesus, Ren. Invasive, much? Asshat."

Ren threw a few pieces of fruit in his mouth and chewed, watching her closely. "You know, I never took you for being a runner, a quitter. Guess I had you pegged wrong all along."

Her anger spiked. Lightning fast. Giselle wanted a good verbal sparring. Could use it about now. *That* she knew. *That* was the skin she comfortably fit into. It was like a tailored glove, molding to her ragged edges perfectly instead of this lovey-dovey shit she was trying to muddle through.

Opening her mouth to verbally assault her friend, her mentor, she caught a gleam in his eye and clamped it shut before she could spear him with a caustic word. "I know exactly what you're doing." And she almost fell for it, dammit.

"Elle..."

"Just stop already. I don't need another lecture from you."

Ren was very perceptive. Too perceptive. It's almost like he knew...

"Well, it's your lucky day, then. I'm all fresh out of

giving fucks about what you want. You're going to listen to me even if I have to sit on you."

She laughed. "I'd like to see you try."

Pulling up a seat next to her, he removed the death grip she had on her liquor-filled tumbler, taking her hand in his. "Why are you fighting this, Elle? As much as that human gets on my last fucking nerve sometimes, he's a good male. And I think he's good for you."

I think so too.

"Why do you think that?"

"Because he actually makes you *feel*. And you haven't done that in a very, very long time, baby girl."

She eyed him, trying to drum up hostility she didn't really feel anymore. "Where's your vestment?" But sarcasm still stood at the ready. It always would.

"At the dry cleaners," he deadpanned evenly.

Sighing heavily and not quite up for confession yet, she hedged. "He makes me feel a lot of things." She meant it acerbically, her tone acidic, but realized after she said the words, they could be taken multiple ways. But Ren would take it the way it was meant. She was confused, torn. A war raged inside.

Ren was the only person Giselle could ever open up to, but it took years before she could trust him. Before she could trust anyone, for that matter. Even Dev. But she could never talk to Dev the way she could Ren. He was a true friend in every sense of the word. He'd saved her ass—and her life—on many occasions, including from Xavier.

"I just...I don't know if I can let someone in that way, Ren. I don't even know if I'm capable."

"That's a fucking bullshit cop-out and you know it. The way I see it, you're intentionally sabotaging this, hoping he'll just bail so you can have someone besides yourself to blame this failure on." She bristled. He was hitting far too close to the truth. "Here me out, tiger. You are not that same emotionally scarred young woman who stood in front of Dev and me, not begging for *your* life, but the lives of so many other females you knew could be saved if you'd only succeeded at killing that preying sick fucker, Siobhan."

Her shame-filled gaze dropped, but Ren hooked a finger under her chin and lifted to connect their eyes again.

"I never told you this—I didn't want you to think I felt sorry for you when the only thing I ever felt was awe for what you'd lived through and how you got out, but you have the mental strength of ten vampires, Giselle. You are a firestorm, burning up anything in your path that stands in the way of your end goal. Turn those flames up a thousand fucking degrees and ash this shit for good. No looking back. Don't let your past pave your future, baby girl. Then, they win. Don't. Let. Them. Win." He peppered the last four words hard. "That human wants you. He *loves* you and you can deny it until your face turns purple, but I know you feel the same way about him."

She had no comeback, so she diverted. "I have unfinished business." Ren knew all too well the personal vendetta she'd undertaken.

After all this time, Siobhan had never been found. Another reason she felt she couldn't move forward with the detective. How could she tie his life—literally—to hers only to take it if she didn't make it through the battle with him? Because there was no fucking way she'd ever let that go. She would hunt him and kill him, even if that meant giving her own life. With the shit storm Xavier had stirred up lately, revenge had taken a back seat, but it was by no means over. It would never be over as long as his heart beat.

"Excuses are like assholes, Elle. Everyone's got one."

She smirked. "Where'd you get that line from?"

"I may have poached it from Sarah. Pretty good, huh?" His brows wagged in smug pride.

Her smile was fleeting before she sobered again. "I'm scared," she finally choked. God, that was hard to say. Fear made her feel exposed. Admitting it, however, was akin to splitting herself open for all the world to see her foul, fucked-up insides. Her black heart. She had spent the last one hundred twenty years hardening herself to stone so she'd never be hurt again. Giselle wasn't scared of anyone or anything.

Except for Mike fucking Thatcher.

Damn him.

Putting his arm around her, he pulled her close. "I know. Elle, you've been evading anything that resembles a relationship since I've known you. It's time."

"Time for what?" Her voice sounded small and meek. Not at all like the self-assured witch she worked hard to build and maintain. She felt as if she was losing herself piece by small piece.

"Time to stop running. Time to be happy." He paused a few moments, speaking softly in her ear. "Time to let yourself be loved by your Fated, baby girl. You deserve it."

He knew.

Of course, he knew.

Tears, those traitorous bitches, stung her eyes, burned her nose. She hadn't cried since she was twenty. Now she'd broken twice within the span of a month. Every part of her body betrayed her mind, including her heart. She was going soft. There was no other explanation.

"He can't know. He can't know what happened to me, Ren. He'll never look at me the same."

There it was. Her deepest fear now out in the open.

Wrapping her tightly in his arms, he whispered, "I think that's exactly what needs to happen, Elle." She tried breaking free but he pressed her closer. "No. Listen to me. He's your missing piece. His love can heal you if you let it. And a mate's love is unconditional. It will never change what happened to you, but he can help you make new memories, good ones, that eclipse the bad. It's already happening, I can tell. Stop pushing him away."

Fisting the back of his shirt, she sank into his optimism. She didn't want to acknowledge anything he said, so she deferred to the classics. "And what do you know about love?"

As soon as it left her mouth, she felt remorse. The chuckle in her ear was warm and comforting, though. He'd let the slam roll off his back the way he usually did. "If you'd open your eyes, you'd see its magic all around you."

He was talking about the Lords and their mates. How each had healed the other in some way. Dev was definitely the least fucked up of the three, but she could see Kate completed him in ways he hadn't been before.

It made her ache. It made her green with gut-rotting, slimy envy.

"I'll think about it." That's the most she could commit to at the moment.

Pressing a kiss to her head, Ren rose and slid the nearly empty container back into the fridge. "Don't wait too long. Sometimes, things slip away because we didn't have the guts to go after them when they were ours for the taking. Don't let regret shackle itself to your feet like dead weight. You're already carrying too much shit around behind you."

Her forehead scrunched. Ren brandished his fun-loving, easygoing-but-pompous attitude like a ribbon. It was fluid, always controlled and if you didn't watch close enough, it created illusions you could mistake as reality. "If I didn't know better, that sounds like experience talking."

A shoulder shrug, accompanied by a vague, "We all have regrets, Elle. All of us. Some just weigh more than others," was all she got before Ren left her alone in the darkness with her own tumultuous thoughts once again.

CHAPTER 5

Giselle

Mike's house was dark again, but this time, she helped herself inside to scour for clues about where he might be. Standing in the darkened living room she was able to see with perfect clarity as if it were midday. Gazing around, the house was unusually messy, as if he'd left suddenly. There were dirty dishes in the sink. A half-empty bottle of soda on the counter. A blanket that was usually draped over the back of the sofa was rolled into a ball and rested on the cushion at one end as if he'd used it for a pillow.

On the desk, his laptop was open and there was a notebook scrawled with information from their research to track down Sarah's lineage. She noticed an address in Des Plaines, Illinois and wondered if he was actually successful at finding something. Flipping through the sloppy pages she could see he'd kept going in her absence. That thought made her unreasonably happy.

Goddamn him and his ability to make me feel anything but indifference.

She couldn't get Ren's words out of her head. *"Because he actually makes you feel. And you haven't done that in a very, very long time, baby girl."* She hated that he was right. She'd functioned for well over a hundred years wielding apathy like a coat of impenetrable armor. She had no use for kindness, sympathy, or longing. Those were fool's emotions that clouded one's vision and erased sound judgment.

Walking back to her Fated's bedroom, the messy, twisted sheets made her body tingle as she remembered how he'd demanded she come again and again by his hand the night she'd snuck out. How she wanted more, but denied them both out of fear and shame.

Suddenly, profound loneliness overtook her and she found herself lying in his bed. Curling his pillow into her chest, she inhaled his unique scent, fighting the hunger she felt for him everywhere. She lost track of how long she lay there, pondering her next move, but she couldn't stop memories assailing her from long ago when her life changed forever.

"I don't want your pity," she responded flippantly. *The Vampire Lord had just spared her life, yet she was lipping off to him like a petulant child. She'd expected— wanted—immediate death and was confused at this outcome and what it meant for her future. If he thought she had escaped one hell to be dropped into another, he was sorely mistaken, Vampire Lord or not.*

"I don't do pity," he replied impassively.

"I'm not going to fuck you."

His deep laugh was comforting, more than it should be. "You're not my type, female."

This was a situation she had not even considered. She'd expected swift judgment, followed by a painless death. She was owed that, dammit.

But sympathy? Pardon? Freedom? None of it made

sense. The Vampire Lord she'd heard rumors of was benevolent, yes, but he also followed the letter of the law. They did not kill humans. It brought too much attention to them. Unwanted attention. And unwanted attention led to snooping and snooping led to questions. Questions that would lead to more death. No. Their two laws were steadfast and absolute. And regularly enforced for a reason.

"There will be anarchy. They'll want my head." She'd left human females husbandless. Vampire mates would die. Children would be fatherless, in some cases losing both parents. The Vampire King would be hunted and strung up for keeping her alive when she'd killed so many others.

"Let me worry about that," he replied smoothly, as though it mattered not when it did.

"What am I to do now?" she mumbled to herself, but the Vampire Lord answered her.

"You will stay here."

Her head snapped up. "Stay? With you? How will I earn my keep? I'm not a charity case."

"Such spirit," he said lowly, contemplating. "What is your skill, Giselle?"

What he really meant was how did she, a lone, untrained female, manage to kill so many without assistance? Humans were easy to kill, their fragility making their lives literally one wrong step away from mortality. Any vampire, even a young one, could kill a human as easily as snapping a dry twig in half between two fingers.

But it took one with skill and savvy to end another of their kind. The only way she was able to slay half a dozen old and powerful vampires was because of her skill and the stealth it brought her. Human minds were easy to break. Child's play. She couldn't use her skill on vampires, but it only took one weak human whom her brothers placed too much trust in to bring *down six of a more powerful species, more powerful than her.*

Her lips clamped shut. No. This was a secret she'd kept hidden from even her own family. No way was she divulging it to someone she didn't know or trust.

"Your skill," he commanded silkily, drawing the words out of her like they were connected to an invisible rope to which he held the end. And pulled. Her resistance was futile.

"Mind sifting."

He nodded coolly as if that unique talent was irrelevant. But it wasn't. She could draw out any thought, any memory, no matter how far buried in the human mind. Even though skills were passed down through bloodlines, hers had a unique twist: when she was sorting through someone's memories, the other party couldn't detect it. Her brothers had not possessed that particular ability and she always wondered if her "XX" chromosomes had something to do with it. She knew no other female vampires to ask, so she'd only ever been able to make assumptions.

"Ren."

"Yes, my lord." The one he referred to as Ren came to stand by the Vampire Lord's side. He was the one to gently guide her out of the bar yesterday. God, he was beautiful. One of the most gorgeous vampires she'd ever seen.

"Giselle is your responsibility. Find something...useful for her to do."

"Of course, my lord."

"I'm not going to fuck him either," she spouted. She wouldn't do that with anyone ever again as long as she lived.

The Vampire Lord rose from his seat and came to stand directly in front of her taking her hands in his. Damn he was intimidating. His presence was imposing, his eyes piercing. Seeing things no one else had. She was skittish and wanted to pull away, but his intense gaze had her frozen with fear. Maybe she'd run her mouth once too much.

But his gentle and sincere voice nearly broke her on the spot. No one had spoken to her as if they actually cared. Ever. "Giselle, no one will ever hurt you or make you do anything you don't want ever again. And if they do, they'll have me to answer to. You are under my protection. Do you understand?"

Annoying tears welled in her eyes. She could only nod, spilling a few down her cheeks. At twenty and fully blooded, she was a grown female vampire, but she'd never felt more like a child before.

"You are safe now." Then he did something totally unexpected and at odds with the ferocity that rolled off him like whitecaps. He took her in his arms and held her while she sobbed.

———————

Giselle remembered how uncertain she'd been during the early days with Dev. She kept waiting for him to go back on his word...to violently use her as the others had. But he never did and slowly, ever so slowly, she began to trust again. In the Vampire Lord. In Ren, his second. And now, in the detective.

Frustrated that she waffled like a teeter-totter, she rose from the bed and began wandering—fine, *snooping*—around Mike's room. Dirty clothes lay on the floor by the overflowing hamper. Extra change, a few crumpled bills, Chap Stick, and three crinkly gum wrappers littered his nightstand. Freshly folded towels sat in a chair in the corner of the room, needing to be put away. His bedroom was different than the rest of his house. Lived in. Messy. Imperfect. She liked that.

Absently, she opened a drawer. Loose socks sat

beside folded boxers. She closed that one and pulled out the next. T-shirts were haphazardly shaped into squares, but the one on top caught her attention. It was a navy tee with white Milwaukee Police Department in big block letters across the chest. The one she'd worn the first night she spent with him.

She ran her fingers over the soft fabric remembering how good it felt to have his fingers bring her to orgasm, breaking her long self-imposed seal. If she concentrated hard enough, she could still feel the tingles that started at her core and spread like wildfire through her limbs, burning the ends of her fingertips and toes. She could still smell the mint on his breath when he told her to come and see the flames of his own desire dancing in his clouded eyes as he released on her heels.

Lifting the cotton garment, she brought it to her nose and breathed deeply. It smelled snarky and stubborn and faintly of his spicy cologne. Jesus, she missed him, the pain in the ass. Putting it back, she arranged it just as before and shut the drawer.

She intended to leave before she did anything else stupid—such as sniff a pair of boxers or gouge the eyes out on any photos of girlfriends past—when her eyes lifted and caught her reflection in the mirror.

She froze at what she saw.

Cheeks bright with a blush.

Lids hooded in desire.

Lips parted on a slight pant.

She looked desirable, bewitching, alluring. Every much the predator she was.

For a long time, she stood there, staring at the woman looking back.

Giselle was beautiful. She knew it. Males knew it. It wasn't conceit. It couldn't be conceit if it was true. But she loathed her beauty. Detested it. Oh, she exercised it expertly. That's one of the skills she'd honed and perfected. Males, regardless of species, thought with their dicks first, their brains a distant second, and she'd used that to her advantage thousands of times over the years. But each time she lured them into her finely spun web, she hated herself a bit more because it reminded her of ghosts of the past.

"You're so fucking beautiful," the rutting male whispered from behind. Instead of listening to his words, she plotted. Planned to cut out his tongue and feed it to him right before she slit his throat.

She'd heard it often and the more it was spoken, the more she knew the opposite to be true. Externally, her face may be striking, her curves just the right proportions, her sultry voice enough to lure any man to his untimely death. But that was at odds with what churned underneath the superficial surface. She was a twisted-up knot of hate and revenge. And everyone knew hate was vile and ugly. How they couldn't see the repulsiveness underneath her skin confounded her.

Regardless of the arrogance she outwardly portrayed, Giselle had lived with self-loathing her entire life, always believing her inner hideousness eclipsed anything else. Her soul was corrupt. Her heart a black pit. Her body a used vessel.

But her Fated changed all that.

He was the only person who had truly made her feel beautiful on the inside, who'd chipped away at that thick black hate with every barbed word, each rough kiss.

From him, that once-loathed word was now a gentle, sweet caress.

She liked it. *More* than liked it.

She didn't want it to end.

Now she just needed to find him, even if she still wasn't sure what she was going to do with him once she did.

CHAPTER 6

REN

"How is your mate, my lord?"

Dev looked up from his laptop, eyeing Ren with irritation. "Have I or have I not asked you repeatedly not to call me that?"

Ren eased into the seat across from Dev, throwing an ankle on the opposite knee. "Hmmm, that sounds like a new one to me." He bit into the shiny green apple, the bitter juice flying everywhere. A swipe of his hand on Dev's fancy desk wiped its evidence away before Dev could jump down his throat about how expensive this piece of wood was. It was *wood*. From trees. There was a whole fucking forest of them right outside the front door.

"Are you trying to piss me off?" Dev retorted, eyes tracking to the smear now marring the glossy top. He held in a smartass retort, but damn it tickled to be let loose.

"Is it working?" He wagged his eyebrows playfully.

Dev laughed. It was loud and boisterous. "Fuck no. You'll have to try harder than that, my friend. And to answer your question, Kate is good. She's resting." Kate was six months pregnant with their first child and Dev couldn't be more overprotective.

Things were tenuous, teetering on the edge of war. Destruction. Possible world annihilation if they didn't put Xavier down. Fast. The maniacal bastard had stepped up his fucking game to an all-time new level and with each new facet they uncovered, Ren became more and more concerned there would never be an end to this evil he relentlessly pursued. His greatest fear was that they'd never win. Every Lord and his respective mate was in grave danger, but with Kate pregnant, the stakes had been upped considerably. Xavier wanted this child, his grandchild. Badly. And he knew the malevolent motherfucker would stop at nothing to get to it.

Their only choice was to stop him first.

"It's coming to a head."

"That it is," Dev sighed, scrubbing his face in frustration. Ren felt the anxiety his leader and friend was under. Dev had a lot of responsibility, but right now protecting Kate was his number one priority. As it should be. The fact they had to cut their honeymoon short and he had to bring her back into the hotbed of danger gutted him. And in turn, it gutted Ren.

"Do you actually think we'll kill this fucker once and for all?"

"We must, Ren. I will not have our mates in Xavier's sights any longer."

Ren had hope that in just a few short days, their centuries-old nightmare would be wiped from the Earth once and for all, but they were in a holding pattern. They knew enough now to understand Xavier didn't trust a soul, including the vampire who was supposedly his second, Geoffrey. And they were waiting for Geoffrey to produce all the information they needed to orchestrate a massive attack on all of Xavier's compounds at once, effectively crippling him for good.

"Whatever the plan, you need to stay here with your mate. Protect her first and foremost," Ren announced matter-of-factly.

Dev crossed his beefy arms in front of his equally beefy chest, his face now turned down into a scowl. "Under any other circumstances, I'd make sure you were *painfully* aware how out of line you are, friend or not."

Yeah, Dev didn't take too kindly to Ren trying to tell him what to do but fuck it. It was his responsibility to protect his Lord as well as his mate and unborn child. He'd never taken that duty more seriously since Dev met Kate just mere months ago. If Dev was a target before, he was doubly now since his mate was Xavier's daughter.

"But I'd say under the circumstances you're right."

Ren nodded sharply, happy he didn't have to beat Dev down with reason. "That's settled then."

"Only because that's how I wish it."

He fought the smirk that begged to curl his lip. He lost. "Of course, my lord."

"You're such a pain in the fucking ass, Ren."

"I endeavor to improve daily, my lord."

Dev chuckled darkly, shaking his head in disbelief. Dev knew he was full of shit. "On a different subject, how's Elle?"

Ren had never seen Giselle more conflicted than she'd been these past few months since meeting Detective Mike Thatcher. Other than Dev, Ren didn't love anyone more than Giselle. He felt intensely protective of her, like papa bear. And like a papa bear, it was his job to ensure that whoever his girl ended up with was up to snuff.

He knew immediately the first time he saw them together the human cop was Elle's Fated mate. Knowing his intense hatred for vamps, Ren didn't like it, but the more he saw them together and saw how she tempered and changed around him as he did around her, the more he knew Fate had chosen right for her. He'd accepted it. Now Elle had to.

"She's fighting it." Dev was Ren's Joe Friday, his partner in crime in trying to push two stubborn mules together. But he'd never say that to Dev. He wasn't even sure the Vampire Lord had seen *Dragnet*. Dev wasn't much of a movie or TV buff.

His leader was quiet, contemplative. It shredded them both to watch Giselle's inner struggle, a daily battle against her personal demons. Ren was insanely proud of the way she'd fought her way out of that hell hole, but he'd wished many times over the years that he could resurrect every male who laid a hand on her and interminably torture them instead. He'd flay them, kill them, then bring them back to start the agonizing process all over again.

"She say anything to you yet about Xavier?"

"No." She'd stubbornly kept the events of the days in his captivity to herself, despite his gentle prodding. But one thing he did know: it had set her back as if she was standing fresh in front of them again, a strong but vulnerable twenty-year-old. Twelve decades of work vanished and Ren's only hope to get back the Elle who had come so far, regardless of what she thought, was that fucking human. The detective was the only one who could fix her. If she would just let him.

"I worry about her."

"So do I. She's stronger than she gives herself credit for, but if she keeps fighting the mating bond with Thatcher, I'm afraid we may lose her for good."

"You're all over that, I suppose."

"Fucking right I am. She loves him. He loves her."

"Have a little girl time with the detective, did you? Because I know that wouldn't have come from our Elle," Dev joked.

Ren started laughing. "I'd say the room was thick as tar with testosterone instead. Fucker went head-to-head with me. Thought I had some nonplatonic interest in his woman."

Dev laughed. "I'm actually somewhat impressed by his stupidity. Maybe he's good enough for our girl."

"I think maybe he is." He actually fucking *was*. Threatening Ren was a foolish and life-ending move. He was duly impressed the thought even crossed the human's mind to challenge a species ten times his strength. It was selfless and brimmed with possession. Elle belonged to the detective and Thatcher had made sure Ren knew. That move, right there, solidified his rightful place beside Ren's baby girl.

"Where's Elle now?"

Ren lobbed the core of his eaten fruit toward the silver, circular bin just inside the closed door. It landed with a dull thud inside. "Well, if my instincts are tingling right, she's stalking her detective. But he's gone dark, so I plan to give her a subtle nudge in the right direction."

"You know where he is?"

"Yes. I don't know when he'll be back, but I know someone who does," he winked.

Ren had always kept close tabs on the detective for many reasons, not the least of which was he knew the cop wasn't leading their fan club. But ever since he became involved with this whole Xavier debacle, the human's life was more in danger than ever and he'd be damned if he'd let Elle lose her mate before she had time to come to grips with what that meant for her.

He didn't profess to know exactly what the bonding draw felt like between a female vampire and her mate, but he knew it was different, less intense in some ways than the way a male vampire felt about his Moira. At least on the female vampire's part. He had a feeling, though, based on how the detective went possessively green at the thought of Ren and Giselle together, that a human male felt very much the same way as a vampire male: enthralled, fiercely protective, and pull-your-hair frustrated at the challenge their Moiras present at every turn.

"One final thing." His voice sobered, getting Dev's

attention. When Dev nodded for him to continue, he added, "I have another lead on Siobhan."

His powerful ruler bristled, jaw clenching, eyes darkening in rage at the name of the vampire who had tested them for over a century. The one he had secretly stepped up efforts to find since Elle found her Fated. He may not know yet whether he trusted that twisted fuck, but Geoffrey was a wealth of information on the depraved, that's for sure. Ren was going to enlist his help if they both made it through the upcoming battle with Xavier.

"We can't afford to be without you right now. Not when we're this close to putting Xavier down, Ren. I'm sorry." Dev looked genuinely conflicted. He knew as well as Ren this was the one final piece Elle needed to put her past completely underground. Pun intended.

Her perpetrator was out there running around, free from punishment for his wrongdoings. That battered at the psyche of even the strongest survivors. He needed to right that ship. For Elle, but also for the many females that demented fuck no doubt had likely degraded and ruined as badly as his girl.

"I know. But after that's done, he's mine. Just wanted to give you a heads up that I may be gone for a few days. I'll be sure Thane and Manny will step in to cover me."

"You know Elle wants that pleasure." Dev eyed him cautiously. Yeah, Giselle had made no bones about the fact this was *her* kill, *her* right and Ren should butt the fuck out of her business. But this vampire was one depraved animal. Ren was confident in Elle's fighting skills, yet if for some reason the tables turned and Siobhan got his hands on her...well, that wasn't an option. And it had zero chance of happening if he took care of the bastard himself. He'd suffer Giselle's wrath a thousand times over if it kept her safe.

Shrugging, he replied, "She'll get over it."

"It's your manhood."

"Not worried," he feigned as his nuts recoiled tightly in trepidation. Ren rose with ease, his muscular thighs flexing with the weight of his bulk. Once they rescued Xavier's current victims and he ended Siobhan's pathetic existence, he had another idea to get Giselle back to the land of the living. It would make her uncomfortable and she would fight it tooth and nail, but he was more and more convinced this would be the push she needed. But this command would have to come from Dev or otherwise he was certain he'd be looking longingly at his dick in a glass jar for the next five hundred years. And he had plans for his junk that did not include fermenting. First order of business, though, he had a stubborn couple to join. "Now if you'll excuse me, I have some matchmaking to do."

"Just call you Dr. Love. Hey, you should start your own Internet dating site. That's pretty damn big with humans, you know. Lucrative, too. You can call it FindMoira.com," Dev quipped as he left, laughter following him out.

Ren flipped him the finger, along with a loud curse in case Dev didn't get the full picture, but at the same time thought, *Hey, that's not a half-bad idea.* With everyone he cared about falling like saplings in a strong wind, he wondered if it wasn't time for him to take fate into his own two very capable hands and find his own elusive Moira.

And all this sickening happiness was apparently starting to fuck with his common sense. Not that he was against a Moira; he just hadn't given his abstract vision of her much thought until lately.

But that was a problem for another day; he had other shit to take care of.

First: Talk to Jake Keller, Thatcher's old partner. Find out when the detective would blow back in town.

Second: Give Elle a subtle push in the direction of said love-struck detective.

Third: Kill Xavier.

Fourth: Kill Siobhan.

Fifth: Nut protection. Despite how cocky he acted with Dev, he was slightly worried how Giselle would react when he dropped Siobhan's bloody, severed head outside her bedroom door.

Sixth: Put part two of Project Elle into motion.

Fucking hell. Guess finding his Moira would just have to wait a bit longer. Isn't that always the way? That's why, after over five hundred years, he was still alone. There was always something more important to do.

Chapter 7

Mike

He arrived at this shithole well ahead of Jake, having driven back from Des Plaines, Illinois early this afternoon. Not wanting to sit in an empty house and stare at four bleak walls that would only remind him of everything he'd lost and all he didn't yet have, he'd opted for drinking and avoidance instead. Sipping on his warm draft while waiting, Mike remembered the day's events.

He'd spent a couple more hours after meeting Bud Clark and his unmarried daughter, Brynne, chatting it up with them. He'd been dying to say something about Sarah. Let them know they had another relative alive and thriving, but he'd refrained. He wanted to discuss it with Giselle first. He wasn't sure what the next step was supposed to be after they'd found her family. If it was anything short of reuniting them, Mike would have something to say about that shit and he'd go down swingin'.

Like all the women kidnapped by Xavier, Sarah had been through hell. And if she wanted to find her long-lost family—her *real* family—then, by God, that's what he'd make sure happened. He didn't know the particulars of Sarah's ordeal, but ten seconds in the presence of that sadistic evil bastard was ten seconds too long. And like Mike, she'd lost so much because of that sick motherfucker.

After getting over the stun of how much Brynne mirrored Sarah, he couldn't help but let his thoughts drift to Jamie. How he'd failed her. Even though it felt good to finally have one tiny win in his corner by finding Sarah's biological family, guilt gnawed his insides bloody and raw.

Jamie may not be dead, but Dev was right about one thing. She would never be the same. He saw it in her haunted eyes that were filled with untold horrors she could never scrub. Even bleach couldn't touch that shit.

Mike hadn't seen Jamie since that day at Dev's several weeks ago. It seemed like lifetimes ago. Would she ask to see him again? If she did, would he hesitate, knowing just the sight of him caused her unbearable anguish?

"I think that's why it took me so long to see you." *Her eyes lifted to his again, the sadness in them heartbreaking.* *"Because I now associate you with them."*

He still felt that crushing blow sitting hard and heavy on his chest. Guilt weighed him down. The only time it seemed to abate was when his foul-mouthed vixen was around. When Jamie crushed him to pieces with her unintentionally hurtful words that day in Dev's mansion, Giselle silently picked them up and put them back together again with her selflessness. When she'd wrapped her arms around him, he'd clung to her, needing her and every bit of strength she'd given him in those few moments.

Giselle gave him things he never thought possible. Her matching rage seemed to cancel his out. She soothed his soul, his constant burn, his aching need for revenge. She showed him there was more.

Most importantly and most surprisingly, she gave him *hope*.

Hope for a future.

Hope for contentment and love.

Fucking in love with a vampire. Who would have thought? Before he met Giselle, he would have slit his own throat at the horrific thought.

Only there was no denying it. Just thinking of the snarky blonde nymph made his lips curl, his heart beat for the first time in years, and his cock rock hard. Her body was sway and seduction. Fluidity with a heavy dose of sin and a giant fuck-you. She was the perfect combination of sensuality, strength, and fragility.

And she was simply impossible to ignore or forget.

After all these months of fighting what was burning hot between them, that battle was old and weary. He was done with it, but he had a new battle on his hands before he could claim victory.

Her.

He'd gotten himself over the goddamned mountain of denial and excuses. Now, he needed to hike back over and drag her fine ass back with him. And he'd do it. Kicking and fucking screaming, she would be his.

But that was a balancing act he was not familiar with. When Mike wanted something, he took it. When he thought something, he said it. He was as straightforward and brash as they came. With Giselle, though, he knew if he made one wrong move, she'd disappear on him. Just like Ren had warned.

Maybe this time for good.

He was mentally readying himself for the war ahead, but he also needed a fucking breather from the work that was Giselle. And let's be honest...his pride still smarted from her vanishing act in the middle of the fucking night, like he was a Coyote Ugly or something.

"Hey, why do you look like your pet just died?" His old partner's voice pierced his thoughts.

Looking up from his now-ruined brew, he answered Jake flippantly, "I don't have a fucking pet." Well, he did but she was far more work than the four-legged kind.

"You need one." The legs of the chair scraped across the worn wooden floor as he pulled it out and took a seat.

"No time."

"Yeah, cuz you're so fucking busy."

He was. He was expending a tremendous amount of energy prying his woman's fingers from the pillar of stubbornness so he could get her in his bed and keep her in his life.

"When are you coming back?" Jake asked. Same question, different day. Since he'd taken his "leave of absence" several months back, they'd met up regularly to shoot the shit and throw back a few beers. They'd hung out occasionally when they were partners but hadn't socialized too often, and he now had to wonder why he hadn't let Jake in before now.

But he knew. Mike had made a sport out of keeping people from getting too close to him. Jake always tried and Mike always pushed back. And no one had made it past those roadblocks...until Giselle. She'd changed him in ways she didn't even realize.

He wanted to be a better man. *For her.*

He wanted to get his shit together. *For her.*

And he desperately wanted to unburden himself from this fucking boulder of revenge that had been weighing him down like a permanent set of cement shoes for the last eleven years. *For both of them.*

He loved being a cop. It was in his blood, but he'd been doing it for all the wrong reasons.

Danger.

Revenge.

Guilt.

Mainly guilt. A feeble attempt to make up for his past

transgressions with regard to Jamie. So he wasn't sure he was ever going back.

"I don't know, man," he finally responded.

"What the fuck do you do all day? Eat bonbons and watch soap operas?"

Jake didn't know anything about vampires. There were days he longed for that ignorance again, but those days were now farther apart, because had it not been for vamps, he never would have met the woman he was now head-over-heels in love with. Even if she didn't feel the same way.

Not for the first time, he had to wonder if what had happened with Jamie had somehow led him to Giselle. And that guilt tore him apart inside because she'd suffered so much at the hands of the devil himself.

"Pretty much. *Young and the Restless* is getting pretty good. Billy's daughter got killed in a hit-and-run by none other than his wife's brother, Adam. Now Adam's gone missing, presumed dead, but he's not. They never recovered the body. It's some twisted shit, bro."

Jake gaped at him. "Wow...you've really gone and grown a pussy."

He laughed. "I've always had one. I'm just embracing it now."

"Waitress!" Jake yelled. When she sauntered over to their table in her too-low-cut tiny white tee and almost indecent black skirt, Jake ordered. "Two shots, please. Wild Turkey. This guy's dick clearly needs regrowin'. And keep 'em comin' sweetheart."

He hated this dingy, dirty bar that some stupid fuck with absolutely no creativity had named *The Bar*, but it was within three blocks of his house, so it was a quick walk home. Old habits die hard. Cop or not, he wasn't about to get behind the wheel after having even a couple of beers. And definitely not after shooters. Plus, they did have decent live music, which was playing a little too loudly in the background.

He enjoyed his guys' night with Jake, but he was also here avoiding one pissed-off female. Giselle had called and texted him several times in the last day, but he'd not returned any of them. And he'd kept conveniently away from his house because he had no doubt she would probably stalk him there. And if he ran into her tonight, he hoped to be too drunk to care if she rebutted him again.

A pussy move? Perhaps. But she'd seriously pissed him off when he'd woken up the other day to find her gone. After he'd laid his soul bare, making himself more vulnerable than he'd ever been in his entire life. And he wanted her to suffer a little like she'd made him suffer.

Yes, he was a vindictive asshole. Or a fucking fraidy-cat. Take your pick.

"To our dicks," Jake toasted, holding up his shot glass.

"May they grow," he cheerfully replied before throwing the burning whiskey back.

Half an hour and four shots later, all heads turned toward the entrance when a simply stunning, curvy blonde walked in wearing clothes that were a man's wet dream. And his fuzzy brain was immediately on alert. This beautiful and deadly creature with the arresting green eyes and porcelain skin was clearly vampire.

A sharp slap to his pec by his former partner's hand had him wincing. "Holy fuck. Who the hell is that, bro?"

Someone who's looking for a tasty liquid meal.

"How the hell should I know? This isn't fucking *Cheers* where everybody knows your name." Although Charlie, the bartender, and two of the waitresses knew his pretty goddamned well.

"Dude, she's coming over here," Jake whispered excitedly.

Great.

She-vamp sat at their table without invitation. Christ, the gall of vampires irritated the fuck out of him. She may come wrapped in pretty packaging, but she was venomous and deadly as a rattlesnake hiding in the brush, waiting to strike and kill its unsuspecting, innocent victim.

"Buy me a drink," her silken voice purred to Jake. A demand. Not a question.

Before Mike could tell her to pound sand, Jake piped up. Clearly his dick was enjoying the potent whiskey. "What's your poison, doll?"

Mike could hardly contain the eye roll. There were so many things wrong with that question, he couldn't even begin to count.

Her gaze flicked to the more than a half-dozen empty small glasses sitting in front of them and back to Jake. "Looks like I need to catch up. I'll have what you're having."

Jake tried flagging down the waitress, but she was clearly enjoying the ass fondling currently being given to her by the tatted, wifebeater-wearing biker dude two tables over, so Jake went to the bar himself to retrieve the shots.

As soon as he was out of earshot, Mike snapped, "You should look elsewhere for dinner, sweetheart."

He didn't know what to expect for a response, but a broad, shit-eating grin was not it. She-vamp leaned back in her chair, rhythmically tapping her fingers against the worn, sticky table. "Are you offering instead, human?"

Shit...should he deny his friend the intense pleasure a vampire bite could bring? Just thinking of how hard he'd orgasmed with Giselle's mouth on him made him uncomfortably hard.

Yes. Yes, he was cockblocking his friend. He didn't know this female and while Mike may be more accepting and willing to admit not all vamps had evil intentions, he was far from blindly trusting them.

"Fuck no. There are plenty of unsuspecting humans—and maybe some *suspecting* ones—you can find. But my friend isn't one of them."

Her nose wrinkled a bit when she answered, "He's a big boy. I think we'll let him decide for himself."

"I—"

He was cut short when Jake returned with a tray of amber-filled glasses, precious liquid sloshing over the sides in his haste to return to the dangerous beauty he thought he would bed tonight.

Shit. Now what?

Just then, he felt a charge in the air. It was electric and every hair follicle he had stood on end. His cock hardened painfully and his blood sang. Slowly, he turned his head toward the entrance and standing just inside, sights set firmly on him, was the woman he couldn't stop thinking about. In the flesh. Everything and everyone else faded away.

How did she find him here?

He almost didn't care. She'd tracked *him* down and that's all that really mattered. She was here and she was a fucking glorious sight, looking all pissed and shit. He felt fury radiating from her across the twenty-five feet that separated them. Her gaze flicked to the yet unnamed female sitting at their table and he couldn't help the slow smile that turned his lips. Green jealousy swirled with the icy blue of her eyes, making them a mesmerizing jade color that he could clearly see from here.

In a blink, she was standing at their table, hands on her luscious, curvy hips. She looked absolutely ravishing in the skintight, barely-there black dress and leopard-print heels she wore. Christ, she was simply amazing. Every cell in his body screamed *mine* when he looked at her. And the possessive vibe and sharp daggers shooting from her eyes echoed the same feeling in her.

"Who the fuck is this?" she fumed. Every ripple of toned muscle she held in check mesmerized him. His cock strained, aching to get to the woman who owned every part of him.

"She's nobody." His eyes never left hers. He was done with this shit. She was coming home with him and she would be his. At the first sight of her standing across the room, his patience snapped. He was done waiting for her to make a decision. It was being made *for* her.

"Why haven't you returned my calls or messages?" Her words were filled with venom, but hurt visibly strained her beautiful pixie features. He suddenly felt like a bastard.

Throwing sixty bucks on the table to more than cover his drinks, he stood, grabbed her by the hand, and began dragging her protesting ass to the exit. Screw Jake. He was a big boy and could handle himself just fine. Hopefully, Mike wouldn't find his body in the sparse trees outside this shithole tomorrow, but he wasn't about to waste another minute letting Giselle flounder in the wind.

"What do you think you're doing?" she yelled as they left the shabby building.

Pulling her around the corner, where it was dark and private, he pushed her up against the paint-chipped wood, trapping her in place with his body. Taking her face in his hands, he pushed his throbbing erection against her perfectly aligned core.

"I'm doing what I should have done a long time ago." Feathering kisses along her jaw, he took her mouth in a bruising kiss. "I'm going to take you home and fuck you stupid until you scream for me, Giselle. I'm going to fuck every other man out of your head and replace every single bad memory with nothing but pleasure. With nothing but love. With nothing but *me*."

Reaching his hands under her short hem, he pushed aside her panties and found her soaking pussy. Without waiting for invitation, he pushed two fingers in, circling his thumb on her swollen clit. He swallowed her moan with his mouth, whispering against her lips, "And don't tell me you don't want this or you're not ready. Your pussy is weeping for me." Not stopping the movement of his fingers, he continued, "You're mine, and tonight I'm going to prove to you that I'm yours. You can trust me with both your body and your heart, Giselle."

His assault was brutal and the clenching of her walls indicated she was close to tipping. Nipping her earlobe hard, she exploded around his fingers, digging her nails into his shoulders so hard, he was sure she'd leave bloody crescent-shaped marks. But he didn't care. *Bring it, babe.* He wasn't taking no for an answer. She was scared and scarred, but she trusted him or she wouldn't be here. She wouldn't have sought him out. She wouldn't keep coming back.

Feathering kisses along her neck, he pulled back and looked into her heavy, sated eyes, once again laying his heart at her feet for the crushing. "God knows I tried to fight this, but I'm done. I'm a complete and total goner and you own me, Giselle. All of me. You've wrecked me for anyone else. I fucking love you. It will *ruin* me if you walk away from me again." Pausing, he murmured, "You are mine. Come home with me." He wanted to say forever but stopped short. He'd already said enough to drink himself into a coma for a month should she turn and abandon him again.

After several tense moments, just when he thought she'd reject him yet again, she grabbed and clung to him instead, and finally whispered the one little word he'd longed to hear for months.

"Okay."

CHAPTER 8

Giselle

She'd agreed to come home with him, but fear bubbled hotter than Hades in her veins with every step they took toward Mike's house. It was dense and cloying and suffocating, and she hated every fucking second of that useless emotion.

"You're shaking, baby," Mike said gently against her cheek before his soft lips landed on her chilly skin. His concern calmed her slightly.

"I am not."

He chuckled, pulled her closer, but let it go. He quietly ushered her the rest of the three blocks. With each push of her foot off the concrete, the mental sludge she was sinking in became thicker and trickier to shove through.

And by the time they made it up the two steps and he opened the door to lead her inside, she froze. Couldn't move a muscle.

She wanted this. Wanted him more than anything she'd ever wanted in her long life. She was tired of feeling lost and adrift. Tired of being lonely. Tired of being scared. Plain tired.

But walking through that entrance meant more than just letting a male inside her body again. It meant letting him inside her mind, her heart. It meant revealing things about herself she didn't want anyone to know, let alone her Fated.

One more footfall meant no going back. Then he would discover how filthy dirty she was. Horribly used and discarded. Scarred. He'd reject her.

She couldn't handle his disgust and disdain.

She couldn't do this.

Next thing she knew, she was spinning through the air and her back landed with a thud against the steel grey siding. Mike's determined face was just inches from hers, her cheeks squeezed between his manly hands. She loved his domination. He was controlling and caring in the same breath. He pulled her back to him each and every time these fucking insecurities made her drift away.

"Whatever excuses you have for running again, fucking leave them at the door, Giselle. I want you. I'm in *love* with you. Every tough-as-nails and every brittle piece of you. No matter what happened in your past that doesn't change. You got it?"

"Get off me." She fought, but it was halfhearted at best. Still, he held steadfast, knowing she was bluffing. Knowing she just needed a little more coaxing. More time. More convincing. Just more.

Stepping into her, he pinned her body between his and the house. "No. Not this time."

She let her eyes and voice harden, but stopped her fruitless struggle. "You're a fucking asshole. Anyone ever tell you that?"

The corner of his mouth kicked up which made hers tug. "Maybe once or twice. But I'm *your* fucking asshole."

"You're not mine."

When his nose dipped and ran erotically down her cheek and up her jawline, her pussy wept in anticipation. The orgasm back at the bar wasn't enough. It wasn't nearly enough. It was a taste. An appetizer of pleasure she'd lived without her entire life. Now she wanted the whole damn smorgasbord, including a big ol' slice of dessert.

In that moment, an epiphany hit her hard and fast.

She'd visited hell every time a male violated her. She'd thought pieces of her remained there, scattered forevermore. She couldn't be more wrong. Over these past few months, Mike Thatcher had picked through the thousand broken shards of lost dreams and unending hopelessness and put her back together, excruciating piece by excruciating piece. The edges didn't line up perfectly yet, but he subtly shifted around the slivers so they would eventually.

All this time, he'd been fixing her and she hadn't realized it.

"I'm yours whether you want me or not, baby. I'll be yours 'til the day I die and no one else's. Not ever." His whispers rained over her like healing mist, each one washing away more remnants of shame. "Tell me I'm yours, Giselle. Fuck, I need to hear it so damn bad."

His eyes desperately searched hers. As she was vampire, she had him beat in sheer physicality, but he was far and above a soldier in all other respects. Mentally, spiritually, emotionally.

He was strength enough for them both. She knew that now. Able to carry her when she couldn't carry herself. She needed to let him. It didn't make her pathetic or vulnerable. It didn't make her powerless. It made her power*ful*. It meant her past didn't win.

Their souls aligned. Fit perfectly. His darkness matched hers, but his goodness brought warmth and radiant light she'd never experienced before. He was the anchor when she floated. He was the solace when she freaked. He was hope illuminating the bleakest parts of her soul.

"You're mine," she whispered so softly she didn't think he'd hear.

His lids dropped in what she could only say was sheer relief, but when they opened, he was all fire and lust. "Say, I want you, Mike. Say my name when you tell me that. You never fucking say my name and I want to hear it."

Vibrations of fear and anticipation skittered across her skin when she uttered words she'd never uttered before to a male. "I want you, Mike."

"Giselle." He dropped his forehead to hers and closed his eyes. "I want inside you so fucking bad."

"I'm..."

Her anxiety swung heavy between them, but he knew.

He knew.

"I know, baby. It's okay. Let me take care of you. I want to drown them, Giselle. Your ghosts, your demons, your memories, your fears, so you know nothing but my touch. My scent. My voice. My safety. My love. Me. No one else. Let me obliterate each and every last beast that's holding that beautiful mind captive."

"Mike..." She wanted everything he just promised. The tang of his vow made her taste buds water in hope, but fear—that sadistic fucker—left its bitter and fiery hint behind.

"Trust. Me," Mike demanded between kisses that were becoming more urgent. "You are safe with me, Giselle. I won't hurt you. You. Are. Safe."

When his eyes connected with hers again, she swallowed hard.

Who wins?

Past or future?

Us or them?

Panic momentarily bit at her, the unwanted sensation threatening to slice apart a future she desperately wanted, but then his next softly spoken plea made her decision easy. "Don't let them win, baby. Don't let them take you from me. Fight for me, for us."

He was right. Of course, he was. He may not have known specifics, but he would. She would eventually tell him and she had to believe he would still accept her, love her. Trusting someone completely with every part of you, including the impurities of your past, was a scary proposition, but she had to. Her only other choice was to walk away again. And she was just plain tired of walking away from him as though he didn't matter when he was all that did.

He saw the second she caved because his mouth was bruising hers. This time, she didn't push him away. Instead, she dragged him closer, needing him fused to her so nothing could tear them apart.

"We good?" he asked even as he was picking her up, wrapping her legs around his waist, and carrying her inside his house.

She nodded, unable to respond because her mouth was now latched on the side of his neck. Sucking hard, she primed the place where she'd drop her fangs deep and drink of her Fated's lifeblood. Her stomach twisted to be filled with power. Her cells screamed to bind his essence to hers.

Mike's palm landed hard on the back of her head and he groaned, "Oh, fuck. Giselle." It sounded pained, but she knew it was craving instead. She could sense how much he wanted her bite. Could feel it in the vibration of every pump of his heart, every throb of his cock that deliciously pounded against her distended clit, making her mindless.

Scraping her teeth along the plumped skin, she was getting ready to taste him again when the air whooshed out of her lungs.

Lying on his unmade bed, Mike Thatcher towered above her, his chest heaving, his eyes dilated to thin points, looking like an ancient god coming to claim her.

He reached back and drew his sweater over his head, throwing it to the floor beside him, leaving him gloriously bare from the waistband of his jeans up. He didn't stop devouring her with his weighty stare for a single second.

"I'm hungry," she whispered in near desperation. So fucking empty and hungry. Her belly cramped painfully. Her pussy throbbed in agony.

A slow smile curled his full rosy lips. "Me too. But I'm going to be balls deep before you sink your teeth into me this time, baby. I want to feel your pussy milking me at the same time your mouth does. This time, I'm exploding inside your wet heat, not my stomach or my pants or my hands."

She could feel the change in her face. Her incisors were razor sharp. The lines of her cheekbones severe. The glow of desire in her eyes bathed her soon-to-be lover and he growled. Actually growled low and long and so needy she almost pinned him against the headboard and took from him what she wanted.

But she held back because she could feel how much he *needed* to do this his way. For her. And if that right there didn't make her fall in love with him, she didn't know what could.

Mike was always concerned about her and her feelings. Despite his cutting comments, she'd always known that to be true. His actions had proven as much, even if his biting lips said otherwise.

"Do you even comprehend how fucking beautiful you are to me?"

Yes, she did.

With her thigh grasped between his rough palms, she thought for sure he would push upward toward the place aching and pulsing for his touch. But he didn't. Kneeling on the floor beside the bed, he pressed soft kisses down the inside of her leg. His hands followed until they reached her stiletto. He carefully unbuckled it before ascending back up the same leg. Chills raced after his fingertips, catching up to them fast.

"Do you?" he asked again, this time demanding an answer.

"All vampires are beautiful. It's how we lure our prey," she breathed on a moan, barely able to stand the erotic nips he was now raining down her other leg. Her core felt unbearably empty and her hips started to roll in a silent call.

"No. It wasn't your witchy eyes or your bee-stung lips or your curves of sin, Giselle. I wasn't immune to those, but that's not what I see when I look at you."

After her other shoe hit the carpet with a thud, he crawled up her body, hovering over her. With his hips pinning hers to the softness underneath, his cock perfectly aligned, and his fingers buried in her hair, he husked, "Do you want to know what I see?"

She did want to know, but she couldn't help the snide comment that ran away. It was all about armor, protection, deflection. Even now. She wasn't sure if that would ever abate. "You see a species that took the love of your life from you."

She gasped at the sting on her scalp from the angry tightening of Mike's hands. He had her head pulled back and up at a slight angle while his gaze bore into her. "That smart mouth gets me hard as fuck every single time, but your words are wrong, Giselle. I *see* the love of my life. I'm looking at her and only her right now. I see the woman who every bad decision and every morsel of revenge steered me to. I see you, Giselle. The mouthy vixen, who, underneath all that huff and puff, is just a fragile, emotional wreck I want to spend the rest of my days fixing. I want to make sure she knows how fucking glad I am that she sauntered into my completely pathetic existence."

An unhurried smile crept across her face. She couldn't even get mad at his dig into her emotional state, because what the hell? He was right. "You're only marginally pathetic," she joked lightly.

Mike's head fell back when he laughed and it lit her up like starlight. Starlight then morphed into a sea of flames when he wound a hand between them, burrowing his fingers under her panty line. He stroked through her honeyed wetness with a single finger a single time before he grabbed the sides and ripped them off with an easy snap of his wrists.

"You're so goddamned wet, baby," he whispered against her cheek. "So silky for me."

He pushed off her and dragged the ruined lace down her other leg. Throwing the panties behind him, he pushed her dress up and over her hips until the leather creaked and bunched around her waist.

Mike's burning gaze dropped to the place where he'd now spread her wide. His thumbs toyed with her nub, coiling the want in her even tighter. When he spoke, the thickened texture of his voice made her gush until she was sure her need was running down to meet the sheets. "I want you," he murmured absently, drawing her juice from pussy to clit. He circled light and slow as the tempo of her hips increased trying to make him follow. The bastard didn't; he just kept talking. "And to be clear, that means I want to fuck you now so damn hard tears stream from those ocean blues in sheer fucking joy. Each salty drop of water will hold a bad memory and when they hit this cotton we're lying on, they will be washed away for good."

She started to say she'd never be free of her shame, but he shut her up by pushing a saturated thumb into her open mouth, pressing it down on her tongue. On a low moan—his—she closed her lips around it and tasted herself for the first time as he continued to heal her with every reverent syllable, every sensual action. "And because that still won't be good enough and because I don't want those motherfuckers trapped where I plan to take you day after day and night after night, we'll burn these fucking sheets together, destroying them for good. Then we'll start over again tomorrow until every goddamned one of them that plagues you is eternally condemned."

"That could take a lot of time. I have a lot of demons," she said softly when he pulled his thumb out on a pop.

"I can be a patient man when I want something bad enough."

Mike drew the wet digit down her chin, her throat, between the valley of her breasts, leaving a damp trail behind. When he reached her core once again, he repeated the same slow seduction. With each swipe of his finger, she unraveled faster. Craved him until she was almost manic.

She now understood that was his objective.

Drive everything else away but him.

It was working.

"You'd better get a burning permit. That's going to be a lot of sheets," she said breathlessly when he pushed inside her sopping center again.

"Don't fucking care, Giselle." He leaned down until they were nose to nose and she nearly protested when he withdrew his thumb, but moaned long and loud as he quickly buried two fingers in her instead. Pleasure was building on top of pleasure, spreading like slow-moving tentacles with each lazy stroke of his hand.

"You know what I want right now?"

Words. What were they? Nothing would mesh together in anything that made sense so she just shook her head. Quite frankly, she didn't give a shit what he wanted as long as he didn't want to stop.

"I want only you and me in here. In this room, that's all there is. Can you do that?"

She could only nod. Bliss crowded out everything else because her detective's fingers never stopped their diabolical caress.

"That's good, baby because that's the hard part. The rest is easy. Now I want your tight pussy to clench hard for me and I want you to come until every fucking finger I have is coated with you."

"Fuck, Mike," she whispered as white lights started flickering in her peripheral and heat gathered in a violent, swirling firestorm inside the center of her very being.

"Then I want to rip this fucking dress off and have you ride me until your entire body quivers with the need to release. Until you take me right up to that fucking edge and you can't stand not having my life-giving blood coursing through you for a single second longer. Only then are you allowed to sink those gorgeous teeth in me and milk both my vein and my cock at the same time."

Jesus.

Countless males had uttered filthy things as they rutted inside her as though she were a detached, inhuman receptacle for their use. Even when her body may have betrayed her, her mind never did. Their words made her feel dirty and degraded, never hot and bothered.

Never like Mike's sinful commands did.

"I'll take your silence as agreement."

She wanted to come back with a smart retort, but she couldn't concentrate on anything but a never-before-felt ecstasy gaining speed and momentum, threatening to wholly consume her.

Oh God. Her eyes closed on a roll. Mike Thatcher had finger fucked her before, but it was nothing like this. This was sheer, reverent, mutual love. His emotions bled into her with the force of a thousand moons, wrapping her in their gentle rays. She wanted to float there, revel in them for eternity.

So close.

She was so damn close.

"That's it. Fall, Giselle. I've got you."

That did it.

She tipped.

She let go completely, trusting him to catch her.

Her body shook and convulsed as bolt after bolt of lightning raced like gunshots through her muscles, firing out her fingertips and toes over and over and again. She felt wrecked. Blown utterly apart. But in a way she felt reborn, not subjugated and used.

Brutal, beautiful pleasure was all that was left behind and she basked in its warmth for seconds or minutes or maybe even days.

Lost in a sex haze, she hadn't realized Mike had eased off her until she felt his tongue pressing where his fingers had just been.

Oh holy God.

It felt so fucking good.

For as often as she was violated, she was highly inexperienced sexually. Oral was off the table completely unless a male wished for his cock to be laying in a bloody, fleshy heap at his feet or his neck to be snapped. And she'd never been taken missionary style. They also knew better than to get too close to her fangs or their voice boxes would be viciously crushed under her bite. She'd never been caressed or kissed or stroked with gentle, loving touches.

She was glad her detective was the first. He'd be first in so many things.

Mike's groan slammed her back to the present, where she should be. He gripped her thighs so hard, she knew she'd bruise if she were human.

"Fuck, I knew you'd taste like this."

"Like what," she gasped. Rising on her elbows she watched her Fated devour her like she was his last and best meal, working against the spiral of want he was delightfully spinning in her. She started to get dizzy with the need to come again.

His eyes swept up, bolting to hers. "Sweet. Addictive. Like you belong to me."

"I do," she whispered on a hoarse breath.

"Fuck, yeah, you do. Now show me."

Then his mouth latched onto her clit and he sucked. And he bit. And he tugged. And he circled her with his tongue relentlessly until she was crying out, grinding against his face with unreserved abandon as her next release swept her completely downstream in a torrent of love and acceptance and hope.

Tears flowed down the side of her face while she rocked against Mike's mouth, each flick of her hips getting slower and less aggressive until she was finally spit out from the rapids into calm, smooth waters.

Giselle floated blissfully and safely on a tightly woven raft of euphoria, truly unencumbered and free for the first time since...since ever.

And while she had a long way to go, with each droplet she blinked that spilled and ran through her hair, soaking into the fabric beneath her, she did exactly what her Fated instructed.

With his help, she began to let the past go, feeling cleaner than she ever had before.

CHAPTER 9

Mike

He watched her give in, then glow brighter than the North fucking Star.

Giselle was blinding and he would never see the same way again. Didn't care to.

She was the planet his moon would revolve around for eternity. The revolutions would be bumpy as hell, like some goddamned worn-out carnival ride, but he didn't give a shit. He'd weather anything for her. He would lay down his life for her. He would carve out his own bloody heart and hand it to her, still beating if that's what she asked of him. He would annihilate friend or foe, human or vampire or werewolf or fucking aliens to protect what was his.

He finally understood what Devon and the other Lords felt about their mates. Protective. Possessive. Animalistic. And fuck them if they said he didn't have a clue because he didn't live on plasma and dissolve into a million tiny pieces to travel.

He knew.

He *knew*.

When you knew within your soul of souls you would ruthlessly carve down anything in your path to keep the woman you love, you were done. Stick a fucking carving fork in you. There was no turning back. "Back" wasn't even a possibility anymore, because when you spin around, it's completely blank behind you as if it was never there in the first place. It's simply a white, empty void without meaning or purpose.

She was now your momentum, the singular force that drove you forward.

She was the idol you prayed to each night before you drifted off.

She was the very air you filled your lungs with.

He finally got it.

His little minx moaned softly. He watched her glassy eyes open, trying to focus on him. Her soft, contented smile was literally his undoing.

She was happy. *Happy*. Because of him.

Giselle was always stunning. So fucking beautiful it was hard to believe she was real sometimes. But tonight, she looked positively otherworldly lying in a glowy, sated puddle on his bed. *His* bed.

He'd been here before, yes, but this time was different. He'd *felt* it.

He'd felt what she did. It was hard to believe or comprehend and he'd been trying to deny it. Each time she gave herself over to him, he'd felt her anxiety and her pleasure. But tonight was a hundredfold over what he'd experienced before. It vibrated through his very bones and embedded itself into the sticky marrow. It hung in his mind, settled permanently in his drawn-up balls.

And he knew it had everything to do with the fact they'd both finally stopped fighting the idea of them, embracing it instead.

It felt phenomenal to see her this way. He wanted more. He wanted it all. Every-fucking-thing he never thought he'd get. And he would gladly walk through hell for it.

Again.

"Hi," she said quietly, that goofy soft turn still on her swollen lips.

"Hi," he croaked.

He was hard as fuck.

Ached so goddamned bad he was positive he was going to explode right now.

The thought of pushing inside Giselle's tight pussy and driving her to scream his name repeatedly practically ate him alive, but he also understood this was the hard part for her, so tonight he was taking a slightly different approach, one he hoped didn't backfire like the tailpipe of a rusted-out junker. Like the night he told her he loved her for the first time.

Mike shed the remainder of his own clothes. Crawling back into bed, he leaned his back against the headboard and let his legs fall open, his erect shaft bobbing against the taut muscles of his abs. His skin vibrated with the need to claim her, own her, to bind her to him for all of fucking forever.

"Take your dress off," he demanded while palming his painfully throbbing dick. He needed some relief, even if his fist wasn't what he wanted strangling him.

Her bewitching orbs widened in surprise and he waited for it. His witchy woman didn't disappoint—she never did. She cocked her head, crooked her mouth just so. "That sounded like you were telling me what to do," she said bitingly.

"I was," he piped back. He let his eyes drop briefly to where her dress still covered her upper half. She had pushed herself into a sitting position on the bed, but her pussy was still nice and spread open. And wet. Very fucking, deliciously wet. "The dress, Giselle. It needs to go. Right fucking now before I tear it off." Urgent need threaded his tone. He heard it. So did she.

Giselle stood and shimmied the tight sheath back down over her hips, covering the come that was slicked all over her inner thighs. She kept her unreadable eyes peeled on him. For long, drawn-out seconds he panicked that he'd made the wrong decision. That he'd pushed her too far and she'd just evaporate on him again.

But *Giselle* needed to do this. He may have issued the orders, but they both knew she was really the one in control here. That's what she desperately needed. She had to give herself to him...know she had the power and willingly hand it over. He couldn't just take because, without a shadow of a doubt, other men had taken from her before. They'd taken something she didn't want to give.

That thought sent white-hot molten rage scorching through his blood until it boiled over and scalded his insides black. He wanted to hunt down every one of those motherfuckers and end them. He wished he could mercilessly and agonizingly bleed them and watch the life slowly leach from their spineless eyes while they begged for their pathetic, damned souls.

Just when he thought she'd leave him high and dry for the countless time with the bluest balls known to mankind, she reached behind and painstakingly drew down the grey metal zipper on her tiny black leather dress. The move caused it to gape ever so slightly from her amazing tits. His mouth watered at the thought of tasting them again. In fact, he had yet to see her entire body naked for him at one time and the vision of perfection he imagined made a few beads of pre-cum leak from his mushroom tip.

"You're very overbearing, especially in the bedroom." The words held nothing but sweet fucking submission. An unknown concept to Giselle.

He lunged forward, palmed her nape, and pulled her close until their noses touched. "You need it. You need one place to just give in and give up your staunch control, Giselle, and know that it won't be taken advantage of. That you have someone who loves your soul and reveres your body like it's a fucking temple to be worshipped, which it is."

Her smile was fleeting and tender. Once again, he felt as if he'd said and done the right thing. He dropped his hold and eased back to gauge her next move.

Anxiety.

Tension.

Awe.

Love.

Heady, fucking, intoxicating desire.

They mixed together and rolled off her in crashing sprays, dousing him from head to toe in every potent emotion she felt.

Mike began jacking himself again, slow and steady. When her gaze dropped to his stone-hard erection and she licked her lips, his control nearly shattered. "I'm going to come all over myself in a minute and I'd much rather come inside of you, so what's it going to be, baby? Us or them?"

When her bewitching blues snapped back to his, he saw it before she said it.

Thank fucking God.

"Us. It's going to be us." Her velvet voice bled seduction, luring him in thoroughly. Reaching up, she hooked her thumbs in the caps of her sleeves and gracefully pushed the dress all the way down.

Her impeccable tits popped out first. Her nipples were the shade of milk chocolate, a shade darker than the furrowed areolas surrounding them. The tight little points protruded from the most flawlessly shaped spheres he'd ever seen. Fucking perfection, she was. Every creamy bit of her.

Ever so slowly, Giselle worked the leather down her torso and over her curvaceous hips. She was now taunting, teasing and if the cheeky smile on her face was any indication, she was enjoying it.

He was mesmerized. In a fucking trance watching

every fluid shift of her sexy-as-hell curves until she finally—*finally*—stood completely bared before him.

Giselle was always cocky and self-assured. She walked with a confident swagger on her hips and surety set between her shoulder blades. Her mouth was fixed in a permanent smirk. Her head always rode high and proud. But all he saw right now was an emotionally stripped-down, vulnerable woman who needed reassurance. His woman was such a contradiction, it made his head spin.

Giselle started toward him, but he held up his hand. "Stop." When she nervously bit her lip he added, "Just give me a minute to drink in the very definition of perfection, Giselle."

Raw desire glassed over her hooded eyes, brightening the pigment so much he was hypnotized. "Come here," he muttered, holding out his hand. Easing them back, he pulled her atop of him. Her slick folds cradled his pulsing dick perfectly and it screamed in agony for relief, yet he held fast. This was Giselle's world; he was just living in it now. No, not just living. Basking. Savoring every second that her royal eyes raked over him like she was barren without him.

He devoured her in return.

Giselle. His regal queen.

She sat high on his hips.

Thighs clamped. Pussy quivering. Body flushed. Breath sharp.

Perching her fingertips on his pecs, she scored his flesh lightly with her razor-tipped nails. With a drawn-out breath, she tilted her head back and her eyes closed in unmistakable ecstasy, but she didn't move. So, neither did he.

Oh shit, it was hard, though. He wanted to move. Just a slight shift of his hips and he'd be engulfed in her hot, hot pussy, probably coming within seconds.

Locking his seed securely in his balls, he stretched

his arms, cupped her face, and tilted it down. "I love you, Giselle. So very much," he told her softly, patiently.

Her eyes popped open and met his. He waited. He didn't know which Giselle he'd get when she finally decided to open that smart mouth of hers, but it didn't matter. He'd take any of them. Wanted them all. So he just waited. "I love you, too," she finally echoed.

Fuuuuuck.

Not what he was expecting.

Now *his* eyes fell shut.

He was a solid mass of the purest, basest fucking joy a person could possibly fathom. No three words in the history of life ever sounded as lyrical as the woman he was mad for telling him she loved him back right before he was getting ready to sink inside her for the first time, making her his. It was almost poetic or some shit he didn't even know about.

When he pried his lids open, Giselle was staring at him with raw, do-me-right-now hunger. The way her front teeth sank into her bottom lip drawing a slight amount of blood and how she shifted toward him ever so slightly was an open invitation. He'd wanted to give her the reins so she could take this at her pace, but it was so obvious she was gifting them back to him instead.

Instinct took over then. Jackknifing up, he slanted his mouth over hers and took. He took her moans and made them his. He stole her pleas and tucked them away. Ate her sighs as an appetizer. He now owned each svelte bit of flesh he passed over. The slope of her shoulders, the swell of her breasts, the roundness of her cheeks, the silkiness of her luscious pussy. All of it. His.

"Every square inch of this is mine," he breathed before taking a nibble from Giselle's supple throat, living inside her low moan. Her nipples stabbed into his chest like pointy diamonds. They needed to be sucked. Hard. "Every fucking one of them," he croaked.

Laying her on her back, he rose over her. Her skin

was bright pink, her chest heaving, her lidded eyes begging. He wanted to do so many savage, wicked, dirty things to her. He wanted to discipline her for endlessly tormenting him the past few months. He wanted to lay claim to her soul, stain her heart, corrupt her thoughts. He wanted to fuck her in the dirtiest of ways, adoring her in the sweetest ones only when he'd sated the devil inside.

Tonight needed to be the latter, though. He needed to shelve his primal instinct to devour her. He'd have the rest of his life for raunchy and obscene. Mike didn't really know how vampires married, but he planned to find out because no matter what it took, she was his permanently.

"I'm going to make love to you, Giselle. Do you want that?"

"Yes," was barely a whisper.

"I'm going to be the first man to do that, aren't I?" he asked softly.

She nodded, hesitant, almost as if she was embarrassed.

He wasn't. He was a competitive bastard and loved he was first.

"Good," he said, his voice husky, before leaning down to kiss her plump lips. Running his tongue along her seam, she opened and he took advantage. He tasted. He gently dominated. He owned her forked tongue the way he did the rest of her. "I'm glad."

"I ache, Mike." Giselle squirmed and writhed beneath him, her liquid curves a deadly siren song to the wrong prey.

"I know, baby. I'll take care of you."

Mike's thumbs grazed the peaks of her breasts on the descent past the nip of her tiny waist to the swell of her hips before traveling to the curve of her smooth ass. Squeezing each taut globe, he tilted her hips and wedged himself between her split legs.

"Condom?" he asked at the last second, hoping like hell she'd say no.

When she shook her head, he lined the head of his weeping dick up with her saturated hole, bent to suck a bronzed beaded nipple into his mouth, and began to ease in. Instinctively, he knew it was going to be a tight fit, but once he was fully seated she would glove him perfectly.

But as she swallowed inch after inch of his shaft, nothing could have prepared him for this ethereal, rare beauty named Giselle.

Jesus H. Christ.

His senses were on overload.

She tasted creamy and tart under his tongue.

She felt like the fiery floors of hell, but also, the gateway to heaven clenched so goddamned snug around his cock. He had to breathe through his nose or blow his load before he'd taken his first stroke.

"Giselle. Fuck. Holy shit you feel amazing."

She was so wet, so goddamned wet and so hot. So tight and hot and wet.

Shit.

He worked himself in and out, taking his time, trying not come prematurely like some sixteen-year-old feeling virgin pussy for the first time, but Christ. He couldn't deny that's what she felt like.

Once he was seated to the hilt, bottomed out, he let himself take in a deep, calming breath. Smoothing the sweaty hair from around her face, he managed to choke out, "You okay?"

Her walls clamped around him and he groaned so damn loud. He wasn't going to make it. He was going to lose it right here, right now. She felt so...shit, mind blowing.

"Yes." She nodded frantically. "Please move. Please. It feels so good. So good."

He did then.

He withdrew and rammed himself back inside, all thoughts of lazy and slow now gone. All finesse forgotten. But who gave a fuck. Nothing had ever felt this good. Nothing ever would.

Pulling out again, he felt every ridge of her silky walls work against his rigid, veiny cock driving them up together. It wouldn't be long. He wasn't going to last and neither was she if the harsh breaths in his ear and the scores she was laying down his back were any indication.

He'd been with plenty of women, but it's as if he'd been perpetually thirsty, always parched. With Giselle, he was quenched, filled. A lifetime of famine was coming to an end as his balls drew up tight and the base of his spine tingled with that familiar itch. He tried to hold back. He really did. "Fuck, Giselle, I'm going to come."

"I'm so close," she murmured. "Please."

With Herculean effort, he held his own climax back to take care of his woman. Gripping under Giselle's knees, he rose and pounded into her like a man lost and found. When her pussy clenched down like a vice grip around his dick and his name fell in a litany of prayers from her lips, only then did he let himself go.

"Now, Giselle," he groaned.

But before he'd even finished his petition, her mouth was at his neck. Her fangs were buried in his vein. His blood was running down her throat. His body and soul came alive. Pure fucking euphoria bled hot and fast through him.

He came. Hard.

Mike threw his head back and roared. He emptied a lifetime of loneliness and longing and love into the female he would call his until the moment he took his last breath.

As he eased over Giselle, their sweaty, replete bodies sticking together and their words of love echoing in each other's ears, he realized something. He was content. And it wasn't because of a vampire's bite or the massive amounts of dopamine pumping him up. It was because of the woman currently wrapped up in him like duct tape. It was because he was finally where he was supposed to be.

Mike had lived with regret his entire adult life. Fucking truckloads of it. It was a thick shackle clamped resolutely to his waist and, along with revenge, it was the one thing he never wanted to shuck. It was his burden to carry. He'd lived the last eleven years in sick, infected, willing martyrdom.

Except now, both of those feelings were gone. No longer filled with hate and self-loathing, he felt blessedly light and free. Unencumbered.

Yes, from the outside looking in, he and Giselle were unconventional. But his entire life had been, so why not this too? He still didn't completely trust the rest of the bloodsuckers, but he ultimately realized evil was born, not bred.

Humans, vampires, animals. They all had bad seeds, but that didn't make the whole lot bad. So while he wouldn't have willingly chosen this path because up until only moments ago he had been weighed down with two tons of isolation and anger, he had no regrets whatsoever at the unexpected and crazy turn his life had taken.

Giselle purred contentedly into his chest, rousing an insatiable beast. Growing hard again, he grabbed her by the waist and draped her over him. Mouths welded together, without preamble, he slid inside her scorching heat once again.

No. Mike had no regrets.

Except...maybe one.

CHAPTER 10

Giselle

Vampires didn't need sleep. Not really. Maybe an hour or two every night to stay refreshed, but they could really go weeks without any and still be highly functioning.

That was one small favor for her kind, for her in particular. Giselle always hated to sleep. Sleep came with dreams and dreams in her case really meant horrific, realistic nightmares. So usually, she'd go as long as she could without nodding off. Once she went a record eighty-nine days. She was practically delirious, mindless with the need to recharge, but that had been in the early days after Dev saved her.

In those days, even the simple act of blinking brought scenes of rape, breaths of torture, echoes of sobs.

The carnage she'd brought upon her tormentors may have freed her body, but it hadn't released the demons that plagued her in the slightest. She'd believed the slaying of their souls, the stain of their sins would quell the interminable screaming trapped in her head. It hadn't. So she'd refused sleep until Ren actually forced her down through utter exhaustion.

He must have known she teetered on the edge, ready to crumble any second, yet he never suggested she sleep. It would be pointless. Instead, he worked her harder the day she was ready to drop than he ever had before. Fourteen solid, nonstop hours.

First came sprints, for hours, followed by a grueling weight lifting session before heading to the martial arts studio for kickboxing, Wing Chun, Aikido, Jiu-jitsu, Keysi, Krav Maga. You name it. They did it. In between sets was yoga to relax her muscles, meditation to focus her mind, and implement training to hone her already deadly skills.

He worked her until she broke. Physically and mentally. Then he held her as she sobbed and sobbed until she couldn't keep her eyes open another second. She slept for ten solid hours and when she woke, she was still in his arms. He'd stayed with her, protected her.

They never spoke of that day. Not then. Not ever. The only thing he said before he left her room was, "I won't let them have you, so we'll do this as often as you need until you get that."

She'd never needed to be broken like that again, but for that first year she'd push herself to the edge of her limits and when she crashed, Ren somehow knew. And he was there. Could be that his room was next to hers and he heard her screams of terror. Could be the kinship they shared she could never quite explain. Whatever the reason, he knew she needed him and he was always, always there for her. She would fall into a fitful sleep alone; she always woke with him cradling her like a child. Then, when she was fully coherent, he would rise and silently walk away. And they would both ignore it when they saw each other later.

Then one day it stopped.

The nightmares faded.

The suffocation eased.

The other shoe never dropped.

The warmth of Dev and Ren's cocoon of acceptance and affection finally sank in and stuck, starting to melt the ice block her heart had become.

She was finally part of a family. A real one. One that would lay down their lives to protect hers. Ren had worked his ass off, but he'd succeeded.

Now it would be Mike Thatcher.

Her detective.

Her Fated.

He would become her family, her protector.

She'd rest peacefully in his arms at night knowing he'd defend her where it mattered most. *Her very soul.* The hatred surrounding him at the mere thought that horribly unspeakable things had been done to her burned her in the most ridiculously charming way.

"You're thinking awfully hard there, beautiful," Mike's gritty voice mumbled.

When Giselle smiled against his pec, the predatory rumble in the back of his throat that vibrated through her made her slicker than an oil spill.

It was eleven o'clock in the morning. She'd been lying in Mike's arms for the last two hours listening to his slow, even breaths and relishing in the lazy rise and fall of his chest under her cheek. Her Fated had been resting peacefully and she was loath to wake him again, but her body ached so damn bad she thought she was getting sick. She had been hibernating for over a hundred years and his impressive bedroom skills—and, more importantly, his unwavering love—had awoken a sleeping giant.

She was like a rabid animal that escaped its cage. Now that she had a taste of freedom—and real freedom was sheer, mind-melting bliss—she was going to run wild. Mike was so in tune with her already he knew it. She'd lost count of how many times he'd been inside her the past eight hours. He was human but the male could fuck like a machine.

"Do you need me again, baby?" he gruffed.

"Yes," she breathed heavily, almost in apology, clawing the sheets back that covered his hardening cock.

"You're trying to kill me."

Her Fated's weak complaint morphed into a throaty groan when she straddled him and sank down, inch by long inch. She had no idea human males could be this well endowed. When she had him as deep as he would go, she started to slowly cant her hips, rolling and shifting until she had just the right rhythm.

His neck arched, causing his head to sink farther into the fluffy pillows. She smiled when his eyes rolled in the back of his head. "Fuck, Giselle. Yes. Just like that, baby." She whimpered when he hit a magical spot that made stars burst behind her lids and her lover moan.

"You like that?" he panted. Gripping her hips hard, he thrust upward to meet each downward stroke of hers.

"Uh huh," she managed on a slight sob.

"Take what you need, baby. It's all yours. Everything I have is yours."

Her eyes, which had drifted shut, flew open and caught his piercing her, brimming with undeniable love. His intensity destroyed every defense she'd ever built to keep him out. With his taut, toned muscles bunching and heaving under her palms, she selfishly took. She shimmied her hips, her tempo gradually increasing until they were both sweaty and breathless. Mindless with the need to come.

"Squeeze that pussy, Giselle. Squeeze it hard. Right fucking now."

Mike took control then, flipping Giselle onto her back. Bracing on his forearms with his hands securely wrapped in her blonde locks, he took her mouth like he took her body.

Savage. Rough. Ruthless.

He was relentless, a man driven by pure, raw need. It

was exactly what she craved. When he bellowed his release, it triggered an unstoppable avalanche.

Ecstasy slammed into her as she took that last leap off a skyscraper and floated high above the ground. She was weightless. Suspended in that spot between space and time like she was nothing and everything.

Gravity eventually tugged, the inevitable fall back to Earth happening. It always did, sometimes faster than others, but this time, she drifted light as a feather. Blowing back and forth easily on the winds of pleasure. The landing was soft. Lazy.

Her senses gradually returned. Pinned between a hard, heaving body and the softness of bedding, she was wrapped in the heady, addictive scent of sex and her Fated.

"I never thought I'd say these words, but think I need a break, baby. My cock is about ready to fall off."

She laughed, the sound muffled in the cords of Mike's thick neck. "I'm sorry."

He pulled back, cupping her face. "Don't be sorry. I'm the one who's sorry. I'm only a weak human."

Sobering, she stroked his cheek lovingly. He was so much more than he saw. "You're wrong. You're the strong one here."

"No, Giselle. I've never met a single person fiercer than you."

A smile played with her lips before she let it out. She was relaxed and lighthearted. Two adjectives that would have never dared appear in the same sentence with Giselle before. "We could argue about that all day, but I guess we'll just have to agree to disagree."

"I guess we will."

"Or we could fight about it and then have make-up sex."

"Woman..." he groaned. "I need some rest."

With her laughing, Mike kissed the tip of her nose before easing away. She marveled at both his fine, tight ass and how empty she felt with him gone, even just a few feet from her. In equal measure, she both liked and disliked the needy way she felt around him. *Is this overwhelming need for your Fated normal?* She wished she had someone to ask, like another female, because there was no way in hell she was asking her Vampire Lord, and Ren wouldn't know.

Mike returned quickly with another hot cloth, gently cleaning her. Though she should be wrung dry, she squirmed under his touch and sighed when his hot breath hit her inner thigh before his lips landed for a sweet kiss.

"I love you," he whispered against her abused sex.

"Are you talking to my pussy right now?" she asked on a chuckle.

Looking up from between her legs, his smile was lascivious. "Why wouldn't I be? It is spectacular."

Peals of happiness filled the small room. "Oh my God. You are insane."

"Tell me you don't love my cock." He climbed up her body slowly, nipping her exposed flesh along the way like a predator toying with its food. His stiffening shaft pressed against her inner thigh and her moan was so loud she was sure the neighbors heard.

"No," she teased breathlessly. *God, is this what normal couples do? Laugh, play, and have fun lounging in bed after countless rounds of sex? She'd been missing out on this for months.*

"No what? No, you don't love it or no, you can't tell a lie?"

"No, I don't love it."

"A liar you are, eh?" he groused against her mouth. Tracing her lips with the tip of his tongue, Giselle sighed his name when he slipped inside her mouth and her pussy at the same time.

"I thought your cock was going to fall off?" she half groaned, half laughed.

She lost all ability to breath when he slid out and plunged back in hard and deep, practically lifting her off the bed.

"Tell me you love my cock." His mouth crept across her jawline. It was very, very convincing, almost too convincing, but she wasn't done playing.

"It's okay, I suppose."

Along with another cocky demand, he repeated the process, dragging their ultrasensitive nerve endings lazily along each other before driving back in. He was so damn deep she didn't know where she ended and he began. She never wanted to find out.

"Say it."

"Mike..." she hummed. She was unraveling. Fast. The road to rapture was short this time. She'd almost reached the top of the hill when he stopped. "What—"

"Say. It."

"You're actually going to withhold—"

"You'd better fucking believe I am."

The corner of her lip curled. She ran a fingertip lightly over his carotid, practically moaning at the kick she felt in his pulse. It matched the one she felt pulsing deep in her core right now. "I bet I can change your mind," her voice purred, dripping with a lure that was almost impossible for any human male to deny.

In a swift move, he had her hands pinned in his and above her head. "Yes. I bet you can. But I want you to give me this."

Except apparently the male who was to be her mate.

"Why?" she panted. *Do it*, her body begged. *Give in*. But giving in wasn't her strong suit. In fact, it wasn't any suit she would ever wear.

"I need to know you're as addicted to me as I am to you." The steady, languid rocking of his hips resumed. But it wasn't enough. Not even close to enough.

"I am. I'm worse than an addict."

"Then tell me you love my cock."

She was smiling so big her face hurt. "I genuinely like it. A lot, in fact."

His laughter mingled with hers. Giselle definitely wasn't a romantic being, but she'd never heard a sweeter sound than that of their combined genuine, relaxed contentment.

Trying to goad her, Mike picked up his pace until they were both panting. She was so close to orgasm, she could taste it, feel it, drink it almost. It was hers for the taking. Just one...more...thrust.

The bastard stopped.

Again.

"I'm not going to let you come until you tell me." As if to prove his point, he flipped her onto her stomach and slid back inside before she could protest.

But in this position, the familiar swell of panic began creeping over her like a colony of fire ants cutting along her skin. Her flesh prickled and she started to sweat for an entirely different reason. This was the only way males took her in her former life. From the safety of behind.

Flashbacks assailed her. They tried to drag her flailing and screaming into their bruising hold once again. She fought. She wasn't there, she wasn't *there*, she *wasn't* there.

Sensing her unease, Mike stopped and wrapped a palm around her throat, using his thumb to turn her toward him. The lines of his face were hard and soft all at the same time. "Watch me, baby. Stay with me. Only me. Yeah?"

Giselle nodded almost imperceptibly trying like hell to blink away the moisture gathering in her eyes.

"Don't look away from me." Withdrawing slowly, he eased back in just as unhurriedly.

"I won't," she breathed shakily. With his encouraging gaze, the dread began to lessen, but it still felt stifling, nauseating. Humiliation filled her to the breaking point. "I...I don't know if I can..."

"Yes, you can," he replied with a passion she'd not heard from him before. "I'm taking this from them. You hear me? They don't get any fucking part of you. I get them all. You're all fucking mine."

Swallowing hard, a single tear fell. He lapped it up, letting his lips linger. "You're mine. Say it."

"I'm yours."

"I want you to tell me they can't have you."

"Mike—"

"Giselle," he retorted hotly.

"They can't have me," she eventually acquiesced. The declaration felt good. Powerful. She'd said them countless times before, but for the first time in her life...she meant it. She didn't want this invisible hold tethering her to the horrors of yesterday. She wanted to be free. "They can't have me," she echoed, stronger this time.

"Good girl."

Mike pressed back in on a long, broken groan. This time, she focused only on him. His ragged breathing against her throat, the flecks of amber dotting his irises, the song their bodies made together. Once again, he drove them up the sharp edge of bliss in tandem, but it was his heartfelt words that started her tipping. "God, I love you, Giselle."

"I love you, too, Mike," she choked. So much it hurt.

"Now tell me you love my cock."

The ridiculousness of his untimely demand broke her in the very best possible way. She laughed but the sounds were swallowed by his kiss of passion and possession. His demand to obey.

"I love your cock," she whispered against his hot, sinful mouth.

"I knew it." The smirk in his tone should annoy her. It would have in the past. But all it did now was make her giddy. Fucking giddy, like a hormone-ravaged teenage girl. Like...like *Kate*, Dev's mate. *Christ almighty. Really?* "Now come on it," he demanded smoothly. "And come hard. I want your pussy strangling me."

She didn't think she was close enough, but when he sank his teeth into the crease where neck met shoulder, she detonated. All she could think of was his mouth sucking at her vein with the sharp incisors he would grow upon their bonding. The thought of him taking her nourishment into his body caused her to come harder than she ever had before.

"That's it, baby. Fuck, yes, give it to me."

His body stiffened behind her and with a low growl in her ear, not only did she feel his release deep within her soul, she felt her soul release into him.

"Am I crushing you?" he asked a few seconds later on a short pant. He'd gone completely lax on top of her. He was heavy, but oh so right.

"No. You feel good."

"You know you're mine." His broken breath scattered along her cooling flesh, pebbling every inch of her.

"Yes," she agreed.

"Forever, Giselle. No more fighting against this." She sighed as he peppered her with kisses from the back of her neck across her bare shoulder. Every one was a promise she knew he would keep.

"Okay."

"Good. It's about fucking time."

She grinned. Her detective was brash and vulgar and as hot as the sun at noon on a cloudless summer day. He had a way with words that both infuriated and ignited her.

But he was hers and she was his.

Yeah. It was about fucking time.

CHAPTER 11

Mike

"Mighty dangerous to be wandering around a house full of blood drinkers all by your lonesome, human."

With some fancy imported Belgian beer dangling from his fingers, Mike turned from the fridge to face Ren. He'd much rather take a plain old Bud any day than this expensive, albeit tasty brew, but this would have to do. Hell, this one beer alone probably cost more than a case of his rather trailer-park drink.

"What can I say? I'm a born risk-taker."

"Or just fucking stupid. Little early for that, isn't it?" Ren's raised, condescending brows cut under his skin.

"Well, in the infamous words of good ol' Jimmy," he replied before taking a long swig, "it's five o'clock somewhere."

Ren grabbed a matching beer. While he popped the top, he eyed Mike with an *I-dare-you-to-say-something* cocky-ass grin on his face. Mike just smirked and shook his head.

The fucker was starting to grow on him.

"See you found our seductress, huh?"

"I told you before, bleeder, she's mine. Not yours." His voice held the blue edge of a flame. He knew Ren was simply trying to poke the bear. This time, it wouldn't work.

"Does she know that?"

His spine straightened. "Know what?"

"That you think she's yours."

"There's no *thinking* about it."

Ren's bottom lip poked out briefly, the corners of his mouth fighting a smile. "I see."

"Glad you got your vision issues worked through."

Ren's rich, deep laugh carried through the entire kitchen before coming to a slow stop. His knowing gaze infiltrated Mike's and they stood in some sort of quiet, weird...what? Camaraderie, maybe? Yeah, definitely weird, but if Giselle was going to be part of his life—and there was no *if* about it—he'd have to come to some sort of truce with the males in it. Like it or not.

Besides, there was something he needed to know and didn't have anyone else he could ask besides the hulk in front of him.

"Where is she then?" Ren asked, glancing around briefly.

Giselle was giving all the information they'd pulled together on Sarah's biological family to Sarah right now, but since he didn't know if their project was common knowledge he kept his mouth zipped shut.

"Around." He settled for protecting her privacy.

"Maybe she brought you into the lion's den as some sort of fucked-up test."

Mike's lips quirked in amusement. He had a feeling the shit throwing would always be like this with Ren, who had obviously become like an overprotective older brother. It was clear Ren cared deeply about Giselle. Before these last few days, that irked Mike, but now...now he had a feeling he wouldn't even have this woman at all without this male's help. So, yeah, he'd play along. He'd take Ren's little "test," since that's what this really was.

Finishing half his beer in one large swallow, he set his empty on the counter, wiping a stray drop dangling from his lip. "Yeah? What sort of test we talking about?"

"Let's call it a...ballbreaker experiment. See how big and tough your nuts really are. An assessment of your manhood, your survival skills, your cunning, your worthiness as a mate. See how long you can last in a house full of blood drinkers who don't care if you live or die."

He couldn't concentrate on any other bait the bloodsucker sneered except *mate*.

Mate.

So Ren *had* known about him and Giselle. Interesting. He wondered how. Somehow he didn't think Ren and Giselle had had a heart-to-heart because she'd spent all her energy over the last year denying what they were to each other. As had he. But if he'd wondered about her friend's approval, he didn't need to anymore. This conversation would be going in a whole different direction if Ren would rather slit his throat.

With everything in him, he stomped on the grin that tickled his lips. Shrugging nonchalantly, he tossed out, "All right. I'll bite. So what do I need to do to pass this so-called 'test'?" *Test* was in air quotes.

Ren closed the distance between them in three long, powerful strides. Standing toe-to-toe, the commanding and intimidating vamp let his hot breath wash over Mike with each purposeful exhale. Ren's eyes narrowed, his pupils dilated, glowed, and with his mouth open in a jeer, the fucker let his deadly teeth elongate in slow motion right before his very eyes. It was an obvious demonstration of how *he* controlled the speed of Mike's death or the length of his life.

Too bad for him Mike was motivated. And prepared.

"I suggest you get the fuck out of my face if you want to keep that black heart pounding inside your chest cavity."

Pressed between them at just the precise angle with the honed tip digging into the thin shirt Ren wore, Mike now held his SOG SEAL Strike blade. The beauty was crafted with AUS-8 stainless steel and held a lethal partially serrated edge on either side, close to the handle. The salient teeth would tear flesh from bone with ease.

Even a vamp's.

Ren's smirk morphed into a mischievous grin, but he didn't move an inch. In fact, he pressed in closer. So close, Mike knew he had to be drawing blood by now. "Next time you pull a knife on me, you'd better be prepared to use it, human."

"Don't fool yourself for a fucking second. I was more than prepared, vampire. Admit it. I caught you off guard, didn't I?"

Ren's grin widened. "I think you and I will get along just fine, human."

That nonanswer was all the validation he needed.

"Did I pass your fucking test?"

He nodded sharply and took a step back, dropping his gaze to the knife Mike held steady. Several drops of bright red were streaking downward, coating the once-unblemished silver. "Impressive."

"I'm glad you approve," he replied snidely. Wiping the blood on his denim-covered thighs, he easily sheathed the blade in the carrying case clipped to the back of his jeans. Ren wasn't the first vamp he'd had to defend himself against. He sure as fuck wouldn't be the last. Mike was so mired in their world, it was as if he'd always been a part of it. Like it was always his destiny.

Now, he knew it was.

"I want to marry Giselle," he blurted as Ren dropped onto a stool at the island. *Not smooth, Thatcher. Not fucking smooth at all.*

Ren didn't say a thing, his face remaining unusually impassive. "Vampires don't marry, human. They bond."

"And what's the difference? It's still forever, right?"

The tilt of Ren's lips was a mock if he ever saw one. He didn't like it. "The difference, detective, is vampire bonding is forever. Literally death until you do part. It's a lifetime commitment you'd better be sure you're ready for, because once you exchange that all-important bodily fluid, your life will depend on hers. Your life will be tied to hers. Your life will be as long as hers."

Mike's brows scrunched together.

"Yeah. You heard me right." Ren threw a look toward the kitchen entryway. Mike's followed. There was no one there. "Would you like me to explain?"

His head bobbed up and down. "Go on."

Ren spent the next few minutes telling him the ins and outs of vampire bonding. He dumbed it down into simplistic terms, even though Mike understood the dynamics behind it were much more complicated.

It was an innocuous act, really. The sharing of blood.

"I don't understand. If it's as simple as exchanging blood, wouldn't vamps just take any human they wanted to mate with and force them to drink? Agreeable or not?"

Ren scowled. "You really don't think much of us, do you? You do realize the female you're talking about 'marrying' is vampire. A blood drinker. Not of the human species." Each clipped word dripped with disdain.

For the first time—ever—Mike was ashamed at his closed mind. If he accepted Giselle, he had to accept all of her. Love all parts of who she was. Put his hatred for *what* she was away for good. He'd done that...he'd thought. But he realized he'd only done it for her and it needed to extend well beyond her if he was going to become part of her world.

"I'm sorry," he said contritely.

Mike rose and walked to the bay of windows overlooking the winding blacktop driveway lined thickly with evergreens, trying to collect his thoughts into something that would make sense to this vamp. He'd carried this hatred around for so many years, it was more than just a growth. It was a veiny cancer twined throughout his body. He wanted Ren to understand why.

"The week after Jamie vanished, I marched into my advisor's office and changed my major to criminal justice. I had planned to be an accountant if you can believe that. I became a detective because of what happened to Jamie. Because I naively thought I could make a difference. Maybe save others from her fate if only I had training, more experience. Six months after she went missing, two detectives showed up at her parents' house and informed them they weren't officially closing the case, but it had gone cold. She was gone. Vanished. It was as if she'd never existed at all."

He paused wanting to make sure his voice didn't crack. Even though Jamie was not really dead, as they'd thought for the last eleven years, she wasn't the woman he once knew and was in love with. It was still hard to talk about. Think about. He would always feel as if he'd failed her. Was the cause of her years and years of torment and torture at that evil fuck's merciless hands. If there was one thing he was really fucking good at, it was carrying around unfounded guilt.

"For two years, Glenn and Elisa Hallow stoically waited. Cried. Hoped. Bargained. Prayed that their oldest child would walk through their front door, alive and well. They truly believed she wasn't dead. So even though there was no confirmed death, no body to identify, they bought a cemetery plot and erected a headstone so they'd have someplace to visit the memory of her. They left the deceased date blank. It was morbid, I thought at the time, the whole headstone thing, but now I think I understand."

And he'd been secretly grateful. He'd visited Jamie's

memorial every year on the anniversary of her "death" with a fistful of marigolds before he got rip-roaring drunk and tried to drink himself into a death coma.

"Pissed me the fuck off that the cops just gave up. I *swore* I would never do that when I became a detective. I would hunt for the lost until they were found. I would fight for the stolen until I thieved them back. I would bring the broken home to their loved ones, even if it was in a pine box because everyone deserves to mourn their loved ones the right way. Then I would mow down the sadistic fucks who thought it was their God-given right to take others. I became an unfeeling terminator of injustice."

The air was deathly still as if even it was waiting with bated breath for what he would say next. Mike had to assume Ren hadn't left, so he continued. Even if he had left, he didn't care. He needed to vomit this burden that he carried so long and so hard. He'd never spoken these words aloud to anyone, and for some strange reason, it felt right to tell them to the male closest to his love. The woman all this hatred and heartache had led to.

"The first time I learned vampires were not just something made up by Hollywood screenwriters was after I'd graduated academy and hired by the Milwaukee PD. I was on beat with my partner. Since I was a newbie, I was stuck with the night shift, of course. It was a fairly uneventful night. We'd had a handful of domestic disturbance calls and a couple of bar brawls. About six hours into our shift, we were called to this one shithole in particular. There was an incident or two there every single week. Their liquor license had been revoked twice already and nothing but losers, hookers, and degenerates hung out there. Anyway, we show up and stroll into the place.

"I don't know how to explain what I felt walking through those doors. It was as if this vile evil hung in the air so thick you could taste it, feel it coating your skin. It took me weeks to wash it off. Sometimes, I feel like I still haven't gotten rid of it all. Anyway, we walk in and broken glass littered the floors. Spilled alcohol ran free under our shoes. Chairs and tables were tossed and splintered like a fucking bomb had gone off. The place was a ghost town except for two assholes taunting a woman who looked worked over and scared as shit."

Mike looked over his shoulder to see if Ren was still there. He was, watching him raptly. Once again, his face was blank, unreadable. He went back to staring out the window.

That night haunted him. Still to this day. What those animals did to that young girl was unspeakable and what's worse...he let them. He had to sit there and watch them tear her apart like two hungry lions going at a gazelle.

When he finished telling the rest of his story, he was sucked back in time, watching it all unfold again in live stream.

———————————

"Well, well, well, what have we here?" A broad giant of about six eight taunted. Grabbing the screaming girl by the throat, he spun her around and held her tight to his chest. Her clothes were ripped and smattered with blood that had clearly come from where they were using her face as a punching bag. With the other hand, tall and lethal ripped the low halter she wore and fondled her bare tit like he was in some fucking snuff film performing for the cameras. He had the most wicked, evil grin smearing his face that Mike had ever seen.

Deadly power radiated from these two like a nuclear power plant. He knew— knew—these were no ordinary men. His instincts were on red fucking alert.

His heart was doing a five-minute mile and he was about to piss his pants right there. He was scared shitless.

The girl's petrified, watery eyes bugged and her fingernails scratched and mauled at the hand that held her, desperate for freedom. Her mouth opened and closed in what Mike could only deduce was a scream, a plea for help, but nothing came out because her vocal cords were being crushed as this sick fuck got off on manhandling what wasn't his. Her face was turning progressively darker shades of red with every passing second. If she didn't get air soon she'd pass out.

Dick one, the monster holding her, licked the side of her face, his unusual eyes never wavering from Mike's. "That's it, sweetheart. Fight," he whispered, but not soft enough they couldn't hear his threats. "You'll taste all the sweeter and your scratches get me hard as fuck."

Mike drew his gun, as did his partner. "Get your fucking hands off her," Mike growled. The men never even glanced at the life-taking barrels pointed right between their eyes.

He soon found out why.

"Looks like a couple human pigs to me. Wanna see how the better half lives, humans?"

Humans?

"Franco, no." The taller one holding the cowering girl commanded. "We were supposed to get the female, that's all. We're not killing cops. Master would have our heads for that."

Master? The fuck? Were these guys in some perverse cult?

"We can't take her back like that. We'll be castrated before we're decapitated," Dick two whined nodding at the shape the woman was in. It's clear they'd been playing with her, like a spanking new toy. She was in bad shape. Almost in shock already. Dick one loosened his hold and the girl started gasping brokenly for life.

The man holding the girl was the obvious one in charge. The asshole stood silent for a few seconds, rolling around his options, staring at Mike as if he was trying to work out a puzzle and Mike held the clues. Mike put the slightest amount of pressure on the trigger. A move that did not go unnoticed.

The fucker smiled. It was ugly. Vile. Beastly.

Time felt suspended. He knew something life changing was about to go down. There was a very real possibility he may not survive this night.

"How about we give them a little show and a nice good scrub?" Dick two proposed.

Scrub? What the hell were these lunatics going on about? Humans? Master? Scrubbing?

"You haven't even perfected that yet. They could end up vegetables."

"At least, they won't be dead."

Dick one scrunched up his face and shrugged one shoulder. "I guess you're right."

It was the look that did it.

Smug. Menacing.

Bad. Fucking. News.

Mike broke protocol then. These two assholes didn't have weapons showing, and he had no cause to fire but his gut screamed if he didn't shoot now, he'd be a dead man. So he squeezed the trigger.

The deafening boom of his weapon discharging in such a small space was nothing compared to the feeling of being tossed through the air like a rag doll. He landed with a sick thud against the concrete wall. His brains were rattling so hard he thought he might have a concussion.

Before he knew it, before he could even catch a stray thought, Johnny and he were each tied to a chair and set in the middle of the room. They had bar towels stuffed in their mouths so they couldn't talk or call for help. Their pieces were mocking them from the bar top, but it was the bloodcurdling scream of the girl that now had his full attention.

Totally, utterly helpless for the next hour they had to watch this innocent girl be destroyed. Reduced to nothing. And when her body was broken and her soul was shattered, they finished her off. They both callously unleashed the stuff that made up nightmares. Their eyes changed, their teeth sharpened, and they sank them into her flesh, draining her dry. Then they turned their blood-red eyes on him and his partner. This was it. The end of the line.

———————————

"Dick two started with Johnny," Mike said quietly. "He grabbed his head between his palms and I thought for sure he was going to rip it clean off. For a few seconds, Johnny cried out, like he was in unbearable agony. Then he went utterly still. His face was completely blank, devoid of any emotion as if we hadn't just witnessed the horrific destruction and murder of a young girl by a pair of real-life monsters.

"Dick one then asked Johnny what happened tonight and Johnny said *'nothing.'* His voice was wooden. He wasn't fighting against his restraints anymore. He was in some sort of daze as if he'd been drugged. Dick two smirked and then he was in front of me, his hands at my head, squeezing ever so slightly." Mike paused and huffed a sardonic laugh. "I remember that part the clearest. I wondered to myself, where's the agonizing pain my partner just felt? Why aren't I screaming? What's supposed to be happening? I felt nothing, except a slight pressure in my head, similar to a headache coming on but even that was nothing compared to the pure, raw hatred I felt for these two...things. But when Dick two frowned, I knew I was in trouble. I knew I would be drained dry just like the girl if he wasn't successful. A sad casualty of some fucking war I couldn't wrap my head around. So when he tried again..."

Mike turned now to face Ren. The vampire was brimming with rage, but there was something else simmering below the surface. If he didn't know better, it was confusion. "I faked it. I screamed bloody fucking murder and then acted just like Johnny. He saved my life that night, Johnny did. Had they started with me, I've no doubt I'd be pushing up daisies under the old oak tree somewhere."

Ren nodded in agreement. "And so would your partner."

Mike stared at him, blinking slowly. He'd often thought that, but it still didn't quell the guilt he felt. When he probed Johnny about that night a couple days later, he didn't remember a thing. Swore up and down it was a nightmare Mike had, wasn't real. He eventually let it go, but Mike had been exposed to the underbelly of evil and he never forgot. It never quite wiped off him.

"I don't understand why they couldn't scrub me the way they did Johnny," he said absently. It was something he never got. He'd always been immune to the mind tricks of bloodsuckers.

Ren's mouth turned up slightly. "Because you're fated to a vampire, that's why. And all Fateds have some sort of special skill. Unless a human finds and bonds with their vampire mate, they never really understand why they're different from other humans. They just go through life confused. Maybe alienated."

Mike took his time digesting that information, trying to make sense of it.

"So, how did you come to the conclusion that vampires were responsible for Jamie's kidnapping? Because humans can be monsters as well."

Fair question.

"You're right. We can. But it was what they said

afterward when they were 'cleaning up.' They were chatting lightly like they'd just slipped in there after a hard day at the fucking office for a pint of Guinness. They mentioned they'd have to find another girl to replace this one to take back to someone they called Master. Then they started talking about heading over to Marquette. How those college girls were easy prey after they'd been drinking all night, stumbling home from a party. One of them said they shouldn't go back because two girls had already been taken from there in the past year and a half and they didn't want to raise suspicions. The other said it had been long enough since the last one, that it would be safe and they should try it."

"And Jamie disappeared from Marquette I take it?"

He nodded once.

"Along with another co-ed a little over a year later."

After a few beats, Ren said, "Not all vampires are monsters, Mike."

Mike. He almost laughed. That plain name sounded so foreign coming from this hulky, imposing vampire's mouth. "I know that now, Ren."

Ren smirked. "Dev, Damian, Rom, the rest of us...we fight evil like Xavier every fucking day. One bad apple doesn't really taint the whole bunch, but it's the perception, right?"

"Touché."

They stared at each other for a long while. He'd never intended to take a jarring trip down memory lane, but now that he had, he couldn't help the sense some bridge had been gapped between the two men in this room. But now, Mike wanted to get back on track, get back to the discussion of Giselle. To what he really cared about. "So...about this bonding?"

The question hung until Ren finally started evenly, "About this bonding." He pushed himself off the stool and headed toward Mike. "Vampires can only bond with their Moiras, so even if they exchanged blood with another human, they wouldn't forge that mating bond."

"Moiras?"

"A fated mate. For us, there is only one true human Fate pairs us with. Some of us may wait hundreds of years to find our Fated's. Some of us never do."

Mike knew Ren didn't have a woman. He searched Ren's voice for melancholy but found none. "And you think I'm her fated mate then?"

"I do." His answer was clipped but not heated.

"And how do you know?"

"Worried?"

"Not in the slightest. I know I am, I just want to know how *you* know." *Had she talked to Ren about them?*

Ren sighed heavily, looking away briefly. "I've known Giselle a very long time, Detective. Well over a hundred years. She's a stone-cold bitch." Mike bristled and stood tall before Ren added, "Calm your shit down. Just hear me out."

With his jaw ticking and his temper flaring, he reluctantly eased back against the windowsill. Facing him, Ren leaned against the solid oak table, crossing his arms and feet, mirroring his position.

"Let's just say she had less than a stellar childhood. She's wound this fortified fortress around the very soul of who she is in an attempt not to get hurt by anyone again. She doesn't do friends or relationships and she sure as hell doesn't fall in love.

"I *know* you two are destined, Detective, because you've changed her. She cares. You've unearthed emotions I've never seen in her before. She's...mellowed since you two met and I know that may be hard to comprehend because soft on Giselle doesn't look anything like soft on someone else, but that fortress she's resurrected has big fucking fractures in the walls now. And it's crumbling the fuck down around her. Thanks to you." He nodded in Mike's direction.

"It sounds almost as if you're accepting of this lowly human detective," Mike mocked.

The corners of Ren's lips turned up. "You make her happy. What makes her happy makes me happy."

He thought on that a minute, his respect for Ren growing. "What's this life-tying thing you mentioned?"

"You really going to do this, human?" Ren asked with a little surprise.

He stood up straight. "You'd better fucking believe I am, vampire. I love her. I'll only ever love her."

"I don't know how she's going to handle this new version of her. She'll be raw for a while, like fresh skin after a wound," Ren warned.

Didn't he know it? "I'm helping her adjust." But he hadn't pushed her to talk about her past and he needed to. They both needed to clear the air so they could take their steps forward in peace.

"Why aren't you asking her this?"

"Because I...I want to do this my way and I want to be sure I'm getting all the facts so I don't fuck it up. And you know how Giselle is."

"Okay then. Here's everything you need to know." In a look Mike could only label as impressed, Ren began describing everything a vampire mating meant in vivid detail.

A while later, Giselle popped back in and stole Ren for the meeting with the all-powerful Vampire Lords, leaving Mike alone to digest everything. But not before he had a chance to ask Ren for one more favor.

CHAPTER 12

REN

"You ever hear of a vamp with mind-scrubbing skills?" Ren asked Dev as they entered his office. Damian and Geoffrey tagged behind. Rom was absent—after the strategy-planning meeting he had gone to make amends with Sarah for pissing her off, which he seemed to do a lot. Ren didn't have a mate yet, but even he knew better than to make his female mad. Vampires may be a stronger, superior species, but it wasn't any different for vampire males than it was for human males. The woman held the keys to the kingdom. Every fucking one of them.

"Can't say that I have," Dev replied.

"Me either," Damian quipped. "But it would sure be fucking handy."

Ren wasn't so sure about that. It could be beneficial in certain circumstances, yes, but devastating in others.

"What about you?" Ren nodded in Geoffrey's direction.

"No. Where'd you hear of such a thing?" he responded, easing onto the couch.

Ren didn't answer his question. Instead, he asked the next one on his mind. "You ever hear of a vamp named Franco?"

Geoffrey rolled his eyes to the ceiling, clearly in thought. "Don't think I have, but it's not like I get out much. Why?"

"I'm asking the questions here, rogue."

Geoffrey just smirked but shut his mouth. Fucker knew he was on shaky ground with the other vamps in the room, but a part of him had to respect Geoffrey's position and all he was willing to risk to make things right, helping them bring an end to the devil's spawn that was Xavier.

"What's this about, Ren?" Dev asked, dragging his attention from Geoffrey back to his leader.

Ren leaned one thigh against Dev's desk and put most of his weight on it. The heavy wood creaked slightly and he just smiled when Dev frowned. Dev was so protective of that fucking desk and it was always fun to push his buttons a bit.

"Well, I just had a nice little conversation with our detective. He said something that caught my attention is all." He glanced quickly in Geoffrey's direction, not sure if he should continue the discussion with the rogue present.

"Go ahead," Dev encouraged. He understood Ren's hesitation. It appeared Dev trusted Geoffrey more than he did.

Ren wondered if he was making more of this than he should. Though after Geoffrey's little nuclear bomb about Xavier's secret scientists and "new" vampiric powers they'd developed, there may be more credence to give it than he originally thought.

"Well, it happened quite a long time ago. A year or so after Jamie was kidnapped." Everyone had somber faces and Damian threw Geoffrey a look chucked full of malice. Ren ignored Damian, relaying the *Reader's Digest*-version of the story. "He ran into a couple of vamps assaulting a young girl. It got violent, the girl didn't make it, and a vamp named Franco had some mind-scrubbing skill that worked on his partner but not the detective. The two rogues carried on with a little chitchat while they cleaned up and from what the detective said, there's no doubt they were talking about Xavier. They talked about kidnapping another girl and said he'd have their heads if they killed cops."

Three sets of eyes turned toward Geoffrey. He threw his hands up in self-defense. "Jesus, fuck. I know nothing about this. Except the cops part. Xavier has minions all over the damn country in law enforcement, and while he's a soulless bastard, he doesn't appreciate their indiscriminate killing without his say-so. Dead cops are not the kind of attention he wants."

"Right. But young, innocent girls are like snack food," Damian spat.

Geoffrey stiffened, ready for battle with Damian. It was clear Damian wasn't going to forgive and forget the factoid that Geoffrey was directly responsible for his mate's kidnapping and more than a one-night "stay" with Xavier recently.

"But it could be possible," Dev cut in, also cutting the tension that had mounted. "This so-called power isn't something that's completely *impossible*, even though none of us know any bloodline with this skill, is it?"

Geoffrey blew out a long breath, letting his head fall against the cushion, almost in defeat. "At this point, I think anything is possible with that sick fuck." He was clearly as disturbed about this as the rest of them, which earned him another couple of points in Ren's book.

"We need to find this Franco," Damian said earnestly, rising to his full six-six frame.

"We're not even sure he's still alive or if he will be after tonight," Ren replied. They planned to end every single one of Xavier's minions tonight except for the young ones they recovered. Finding this Franco would be like recovering a single gold bar at the bottom of the Pacific without any sonar. Who the hell knew where he was. Hell, he was probably dust by now. Didn't seem to him that many vamps had a long life span with Xavier as their "Master."

"I don't want us distracted by this tonight. If we stumble across him, we capture him. But I don't want anyone's life in danger," Dev stated. "We don't know anything about this power or its effectiveness or side effects. It's too...dangerous. Too unknown. In fact, it would probably be best if he was eliminated." He paused, pinning Geoffrey with a concerned look. "If you make it through this next week alive, rogue, I want you to put out some feelers just in case. We have no idea what the fuck Xavier has set loose with his experiments."

"Of course." Geoffrey nodded respectfully.

"I'm outie," Damian announced, striding toward the door. "I need to spend some time with my mate before tonight's bloody battle." In other words, he needed to do the horizontal bopty-bop.

"Damian," Dev called. Damian stopped and threw a look over his shoulder. "Good luck tonight."

Damian hesitated. He opened his mouth but swallowed whatever it was he was going to say. Tonight would be a hard-fought bloodbath. They all knew it. None of them were cocky enough to guarantee they would be coming home afterward, even Damian, the King of Cock. Rephrase (because he didn't need that visual). *Arrogance.* King of *Arrogance.* "You too," Damian replied in a low voice. Then he was gone, leaving the three of them.

"You sure you're all set for tonight?" Ren asked Dev. Thane, Manny, and Giselle would stay back with Dev and the Lords' mates. Ren needed to protect his leader, but it was equally—or more—important to protect the Lords' females.

"You act like I'm not capable of caring for my mate," Dev snapped.

He was pissed.

Ren didn't care.

"And you act like I shouldn't be doing my job. My lord," he tacked on, though it lacked the respect it should have. There's no one besides Kate who could get away with talking to the Midwest Regent Vampire Lord like Ren did. But that's what over three hundred loyal years together bought him. Carte blanche.

"Ren." Dev sighed, shaking his head. Skirting around his desk, he clasped his hand on Ren's shoulder, squeezed, and said, "Be careful tonight."

Huh. Not what he was expecting.

"Would you miss me if I didn't return, my lord?" Ren's smirk was wiped away when the mood perceptibly shifted to one he knew would be a "bro moment." *Shit.* He didn't feel completely comfortable with those. Okay, truth? Hives. It gave him hives.

Dev inched slightly closer to Ren. Because Ren stood just about an inch above him, Dev had to shift his eyes upward to meet Ren's. "More than you know."

The moment seemed to stretch on forever, and memory after memory together with his best friend slammed into him like a speeding freight train. He loved Dev like a brother. Hell, he *was* his brother for all it mattered. And even the fleeting thought these were their last seconds together hit him hard in the chest. Then it passed and he could breathe again without his lungs being constricted.

"Don't worry." His signature smirk was back as he clasped Dev on the opposite shoulder. "I'll be around another three hundred years to keep you on your toes."

"You mean be a pain in my ass," Dev corrected, his own smile playing on his lips.

"Of course, that's what I meant. Regarding the other matter we discussed earlier, is…" He paused, realizing Geoffrey was still in the room. Fucking great. Now his "bro moment" had a witness. Just what he needed. "Is everything set?" he finished.

Ren hadn't seen Elle in three days until today. Not since he *may* have happened to drop a hint where she would be able to find her detective. And since he hadn't seen or heard from her, he knew the cop had finally, finally managed to snare her. Finding him here this afternoon was just the icing on the cake that was already baked. So, he put the second phase of his little Project Elle into motion and Dev was going to help. Actually, Ren hadn't given him much choice.

"Yes, it's set. I had to do a lot of convincing with Kate, but when tonight is over, I'll talk to Elle."

"Perfect."

"You sure this is a good idea?" Dev hedged. He was as worried about Elle's reaction as Ren was.

"Good? Eh. Necessary? Absolutely."

"Okay then. I'll support you. Now if you'll excuse me, I'm going to check on Kate. Make sure she's resting comfortably."

"Of course, my lord." Dev gave him a brief smile that held all the unspoken words between them. Then he, too, was gone.

Turning his attention to Geoffrey, who still sat quietly on the couch not even pretending he wasn't listening to the last ten minutes of conversation, he said, "You're going to help me with something." The rogue simply raised his brows in response.

The first two "to-dos" on Ren's list had now been ticked off. Uniting Elle and her mate. And after the enlightening convo in the kitchen with Mike Thatcher, he knew their official bonding countdown clock had started ticking.

Now, tonight they would scratch off another. Annihilating Xavier. He felt victory already vibrating in his bones. Tonight it would end, he was sure of it. Then he was headed out to track Siobhan like the fucking animal he was and Geoffrey was going to help.

Ren was removing this excuse from Elle's plate. Not

one person on the face of this planet deserved happiness like she did.

Not one.

"Here's what I need," he said, taking a seat beside a once enemy who had suddenly become a very valuable asset in more ways than one.

CHAPTER 13

Giselle

"What's the matter, baby?" Mike purred in her ear.

What's the *matter*?

What's the matter?

The matter is she's stuck babysitting a bunch of brats when she should be in the fray. Fighting. Killing. Severing heads, limbs. Cutting out sin-stained hearts. Relishing in screams of mercy that are fruitless. But *noooooo*. Here she sits with Kate, Analise, and Sarah instead, watching—wait for it—Real fucking Housewives of fucking Orange County.

Who in their right mind voluntarily watches this garbage? Who gives two shits about haughty, rich, silicone-filled, clawed bitches who spend their days going to the spa, drinking wine, and spreading gossip like a virus? She had half a mind to find these women and put them—and the rest of the country—out of their misery. This right here? This was real torture. Worse than half the shit she'd been through.

The three queens "oooooohhhhhed" at some particularly snarky comment that someone named Shannon had just made about someone named Vickie making up some cancer story about someone named Brooks.

Good fucking God. Shoot her. Now.

"Nothing," she replied tersely. The chuckle that danced over her neck pissed her off but made her heart race at the same time.

"You're a terrible liar, baby." He planted a soft kiss in the space right below her ear, making her hum.

"Stop that." She tried pulling out of his hold, but he only gripped harder, yanking her back into him. He wound his arms completely around her waist and laced his hands together.

They were standing in the back corner of the main living room. She had no idea why she even stayed in this room, except for the fact she felt loyal to Dev. This is where he was, sitting on the couch with his "bride," watching this drivel with her, so this is where she would be. Protecting him. Protecting *her*. Protecting their heir.

"Relax," he whispered against the shell of her ear.

Giselle sagged a bit against the hard plane of Mike's chest and just the press of their bodies together made her thoughts stray to bonding with him, something she'd been thinking about constantly.

As with male vampires, female vampires only bonded for life with humans. Only when a female vampire found her mate, it was quite different than for a male vampire. Males were a little more *aggressive* when they found their Moiras. Viciously possessive, stopping at nothing to make them theirs. She'd watched that play out over and over again with the Lords. And it was really quite amusing watching each of them squirm like worms dangling on the end of a hook. Their mates were feisty, each one giving them a run for their money. Even the mild-mannered Kate.

But for females, in some big cosmic fuck-you, it was very much like the way human females let their emotions rule their hearts...and vaginas. Oh, the physical was still there, as her dampness between her thighs would attest, but feelings were in the proverbial driver's seat. How she wished it were more physical than emotional, because Giselle did *not* do touchy-feely shit. Well, with anyone but her Fated, that was.

Giselle always thought male and female vampires differed when it came to finding their mates because males found the one person in the world they'd be able to procreate with. Female vampires couldn't procreate. It was some sick, warped game the Universe played with their kind, but Giselle hadn't given it one thought—*ever*—until she met Mike.

In fact, brats were never in her five-hundred-year road map whether she wanted them to be or not. And for the first time since she could form a thought, she was angry about that. Mike deserved kids if that's what he wanted. He would be a good father, a great teacher. She, on the other hand, would make a shitty mammi. She knew that, but still. Shouldn't *she* get to make that choice instead of it being made for her by some unknown God-like entity who supposedly ruled their destiny? Would Mike even want her if he knew she couldn't have children?

She had a lot of baggage. Fuckloads of it. Was it fair to saddle him with her shit, too, when it was hard enough to carry on her own? With her inadequacies and defects? Plus he had his own demons to deal with. Why would he want hers added to the pile?

And then, of course, there was still Siobhan.

Her heart sank.

Giselle had come so far in the last few days. Accepting this thing between her and Mike. Climbing into his bed. Letting him command her, love her, *make* love to her. Lying in the safety of his arms for the past few days, she'd almost convinced herself that the rainbow was real and there was a genuine treasure at the end of it. But the mountains she had yet to cross to get to the gold suddenly felt like the Alps. They seemed insurmountable.

Everything she'd never wanted was within her grasp, yet it was all an illusion, wasn't it? Another distorted, fucking trick of the mind. Giving her a taste of a life she could have but wouldn't.

Kate's laughter dragged her from her dark, building thoughts. She watched Dev's mate rub her baby-swollen belly, an act that seemed to click along in slow motion. Dev noticed and his hand joined hers, his heartfelt smile slicing Giselle to ribbons. It was a miracle she would never experience. It was something Mike would never experience with her. The intimate connection between the three of them—mother, father, and baby—was palpable and undeniable and so real it made her ache in places she thought long shriveled up.

"Oh my God, can you believe her?" Kate squealed about something on the show, nudging Dev who just grunted.

Suddenly she was filled with rage. A horribly violent energy coiled in her and it had to be released, so she took it out on the easiest target. Not smart, but whatever. "Jesus fucking Christ, you would think someone with a PhD would want to watch a show that actually developed brain cells instead of killing them." The caustic words burned the skin from her tongue. As they fell off, she immediately wished she could call them back.

Dev dropped his arm from a stricken Kate. His eyes burned and his jaw ticked back and forth with justifiable anger, but he needn't have said a word. His rage rang in her ears clearly. It was deafening.

"I need to use the washroom," she said.

Using her own strength to break Mike's hold, she fled the damning eyes of everyone in that room. After she splashed some cold water on her face, she stared at her reflection in the mirror.

Time ticked slowly by.

The female she saw was no longer the beautiful face of an ice-cold, impenetrable bitch, but the very definition of weak. Loving Mike made her strong in so many ways, but weak in so many others. Pent-up emotions had finally bled through that thick skin of hers, now sitting on the surface for everyone to see and judge. She loathed it. It made her act in ways she would have never acted before. What's worse, it made her regret them.

With a heavy sigh, she dried herself off. Not ready to face their pitiful stares or scathing whispers, Giselle wandered into the kitchen to pour herself a drink.

She'd fully expected Mike to follow her, try to comfort her, maybe even try to fuck some sense into her in some remote part of the house. But maybe he knew her better than she thought because she still needed a moment or two alone to find the words "I'm sorry" that swam somewhere deep in her muddy depths. They were there somewhere; she just had to dig them up and wash them off. They weren't used very often.

She heard the pitter patter of feet approach. Knew by the cadence it wasn't Mike—or Dev for that matter. So, with vodka in hand, she waited. Moments later Sarah entered.

Sarah paused, glanced at her drink then back at her face. Giselle intentionally tried to keep it blank, indifferent. But Sarah...Sarah was perceptive. There was something in Sarah she had liked immediately. She'd even bantered lightly with her earlier today. She wouldn't call Sarah a "friend," since, well, she had no friends besides Ren. But sadly what she had with Sarah bordered as close to a friendship as she'd ever had with another female.

With hand on hip, Sarah started in on her and, honestly, she'd have thought less of her if she hadn't. She would never admit it, though.

"Why do you hate Kate so much?"

"I don't *hate* her." Per se. She just didn't *care* for her. And it wasn't even that anymore. It was just...

"Fine. Why do you dislike her so much?"

Giselle took a sip of her straight Grey Goose before she quipped, "Is this like a Taylor Swift moment or something?"

"Jesus. Drop the raving lunatic bitch act for ten minutes and have a real grown-up conversation for once, Giselle."

Ouch. That barb actually stung. She steeled her spine, but it felt a little melty under Sarah's intuitive stare.

"I don't really dislike her. Not that much, anyway."

"Go on," Sarah urged.

"Go on? What is this exactly? I mean I talk to you a few times, do you a little favor by finding your long-lost family, and suddenly you think you can just ask prying, personal questions. What the fuck is up with that? Do you think we're friends or something?"

"Yes," Sarah stated flatly. She sounded like she really meant it.

"Well, we're fucking not."

Sarah walked toward her, all the while spewing garbage. "We so are, and as far as I know, I'm the only female friend you have so you'd better not screw this up."

"I don't need friends, little girl."

"Yes, you do." Sarah slowly smiled. "I have your number, Giselle."

"And what number is that?" Giselle downed the rest of her drink in one swallow, slamming the glass tumbler on the marble countertop so hard she was surprised it didn't shatter.

"The right one. Stop getting off topic. What's up with you and Kate?"

"Why do you care?"

Sarah crossed her arms. "Because she's my sister, and believe it or not, you're hurting her feelings."

Giselle laughed. "I don't really give a shit if I'm hurting her sensitive little feelings or not." But...she did. She was actually sorry the instant the words left her mouth and it wasn't because of Dev. It was because they were intentionally mean and Kate had done nothing to deserve them. She never had. They may not be friends, maybe never would be, but Kate was always respectful of Giselle. Her love for Dev was boundless. She was good for him. Made him happy.

"Okay, then. What about Dev. Do you care if you hurt him?"

"You know I do." She sighed. Knowing Sarah wasn't going to leave until she had her say, she walked to the oak table and sat.

"Hurting Kate hurts Dev."

Silence.

"You know," Sarah droned as she joined her at the table, "if I didn't know better, I'd say you were jealous. Not in the I-can-never-have-him-in-my-bed kind of way, but more in an I-want-what-she-has kind of way. Mate, *baby*, white picket fence."

Giselle stiffened, anger boiling again. But this time, it was at herself for being so goddamned transparent. Being a frozen, uncaring female was a helluva a lot easier than this right here.

"But since you're *not* the jealous type, then that certainly can't be it, can it?"

Giselle flattened her palms on the table, pushing herself up. "First, I fucking hate the color white. It's not even a color for Christ's sake. It's the base all other colors start from. And second, I have a mate, I will have you know. But even if I didn't, that's not my issue with Kate."

Her issue was with *her*, not Kate. It always had been.

There was a smug look on Sarah's face she wanted to clean up. "And third?"

"This ridiculous conversation is over," she spat.

She was almost home free when Sarah's cheery voice chased her. "Good talk. I'm here anytime you're up for more soul bearing. Maybe we can have a girls' night next week?"

Giselle punched her middle finger in the air and the ring of Sarah's laugh followed her long after she walked away. Unfortunately, so did the smile on her lips as she reentered the living room to make amends with Dev, but more importantly...his mate. She may not have solved the bonding problem in the time she was gone, but there was one thing she could fix.

It was time to stop projecting her feelings on everyone else around her. She didn't know how that would work exactly, but she was willing to give it a try.

CHAPTER 14

Mike

Yesterday was a great day. Fantastic, really. They had accompanied Sarah and Rom to Bud Clark's house—he was Sarah's grandfather. Mike was still riding that high, thrilled as hell he'd been able to reunite Sarah with her family. It was a surprise he thought may put Bud six-feet under, given his age, but Bud beamed like a kid on Christmas morning. Happy to have a piece of his daughter he never knew existed. Giselle bitched the entire time and tried to seem unaffected. He knew better. He caught the small grin on her face while she watched the reunion, but scowled when she caught him looking.

She wanted to be part of something bigger, no matter what she said, no matter how she acted. He was bound and determined to make that happen.

"You seem nervous," he soothed. Reaching across the console of his car, he plucked Giselle's hand from her lap and twined their fingers together.

She scoffed. "I'm not nervous."

He smiled. "I think I'm going to have to invoke a punishment for every lie you tell." He brought her hand to his mouth, nibbling on her knuckles. She tried pulling away. He didn't let her. "There's nothing to be nervous about, baby."

Giselle finally pulled her gaze from the front window and looked over at him. Without thought, he cupped her cheek. Bringing her lips to his, he coaxed a kiss from her. He wanted her so fucking bad. Every time he laid a finger on her, he could think of almost nothing else but ripping her clothes off and burying himself inside her for eternity. A million nights with her in his arms would never be enough.

But after the other night at Dev's when she had her little meltdown, he felt her slipping away again. Oh, she apologized to Kate and Dev, contritely even, but she'd started her slow retreat. Barriers were being re-resurrected. He was bound and determined to sledgehammer them the fuck down once and for all. He needed to push. She needed to break. And it needed to happen soon because he was tired of sitting on the sidelines that had become his life.

So he'd taken matters into his own hands. Today was part of that plan. Pushing her boundaries was part of that plan. Making her *uncomfortable* was part of that plan.

"What kind of punishment are we talking about?" she purred against his lips.

"Hmmm, I was thinking you would have to cook."

She leaned back, her perfectly smooth forehead wrinkled in confusion. "Cook? That sounds like more of a punishment for you than me."

Giselle did not cook. In fact, Giselle didn't even know how to boil water until he showed her. She burned toast. Every. Single. Time. He couldn't leave her alone in the kitchen for fear she'd burn his meager house to the ground.

"Huh. You may be right there. I didn't think that through. Guess I'll just have to tie you to my bed until I figure out something more suitable, yeah?"

Running a black-painted fingertip down the center of his chest, she hummed, "You could try." Jesus, her simple tease dripped seduction. It pooled around his cock, drenching him in highly inappropriate thoughts. Like unzipping and having her suck him off right here, in front of his mother's house.

"I'm sure Ren or Dev would have something that could be used to hold you at my mercy."

Her finger froze just centimeters from his denim-strangled dick. Her eyes flicked back to his. "You wouldn't dare."

Leaning forward until he could mold her lips to his if he wanted, he said in an even, promising voice, "Try me, beautiful."

Her eyes closed in forfeit. "Fine. I'm nervous. Happy?"

"Yes." After a quick peck, he exited the car. She sat stock-still, staring straight ahead. They didn't travel in his car much, but when they did, she liked to open her own door, insisting chivalry never really gained momentum as everyone claimed. She was a trip, his Giselle.

Door open, he held out his hand. She looked at it as if it would bite but tentatively took it. As soon as she stood in front of him, he backed her up against the cold metal, taking her gorgeous face between his calloused palms.

"You act like we're heading to see the great and powerful Oz asking for a balloon ride home. She's a sixty-five-year-old lady who's hard of hearing, loves *Wheel of Fortune*, and plays a mean game of bridge every Tuesday night at the senior center. You could eat her for lunch." He laughed at his unintentional joke. "But don't. Please."

That cracked a smile from her. "But she's your mother. The most important woman in your life and I've..." Her eyes shifted over his shoulder, staring at his mother's simple home.

"*You're* the most important woman in my life, Giselle. Now what are you afraid of?" he coaxed softly.

Their gazes met again. He saw insecurity swimming around, making nice little laps that rippled her ocean blues. He felt it, too. In fact, every day he spent with her, he could feel her emotions stronger than the day before. He wondered if it was the same for her. "I've never met a mother before. And I'm not exactly the type of girl you take home to Mama."

The grin on his face felt like it stretched to the next county. She wanted his mother to *like* her. Giselle actually *cared* what another human being thought of her. She'd come so damn far.

"She's gonna love you, baby. Come on." Before she had a chance to protest, he grabbed her hand and dragged her up the cracked driveway. When Edna Thatcher answered the door within five seconds of his knock, he knew she'd been watching them from the dining room window.

"Mom, hi." He enveloped her slight five-foot-two frame into his large six-foot-two body, hugging the woman he hadn't seen in far too long. She looked older but good. He hadn't realized how much he'd missed her until just now. "Mom"—he snuck an arm around Giselle's waist and pulled her close—"this is Giselle." He wanted to say, "my soon-to-be wife," but he didn't dare spring that on her in front of his mother. She was already stressed enough.

Giselle stiffly stuck out her hand, mumbling politely, "It's nice to meet you, Mrs. Thatcher," but his mother wasn't having any of that. She was a hugger, that one. She reached out and tugged Giselle into her, wrapping her tiny arms around Giselle's tiny waist. He had to stifle a laugh when Giselle looked over her shoulder at him in mock horror. Well, it probably wasn't mock. It was actual horror. Outside of him, he knew Giselle didn't like people to touch her.

"Well, look at you. You're stunning," his mother praised after she'd finally released his future mate. And by released, she was no longer hugging her, but holding her by the arms, inspecting her from head to toe. Edna Thatcher was bold and brash and said it like she meant it. He got that from her.

"Uh, thank you."

"Well, come on in now. I haven't seen my boy for what seems like years and we have a lot of catching up to do." She scurried into the house. They had no choice but to follow or be left behind.

"I can't believe you didn't tell me that," Giselle chastised him as they drove down the highway. An occasional streetlight would briefly infiltrate the darkness that surrounded them, making her glow like a fallen angel.

Giselle was right. In hindsight, he probably should have warned her. In his thirty-three years, he hadn't brought a woman home. Except once. He should have known his mother would call him out on it in front of her.

"So," Edna started, her hawk-like gaze pinned on Giselle, "do you know you're only the second woman my Michael has ever brought home?"

When Giselle's panicked eyes flew to his, he'd felt his skin go a little hot and tried cutting his mom off at the pass. Too late. The words were already out before he could stop them.

"Her name was Jamie, right? The one that went missing?"

Fuck. Hashtag fail right there.

"I'm sorry. I just got caught up in the excitement and I forgot." He should have handled the whole thing differently. Told his mom not to mention Jamie. Even though his entire heart belonged to Giselle, Jamie was still an uncomfortable, unspoken wedge between them, which was why he needed to remove it. Just one more hurdle in their string they both had to jump.

After they'd moved past the elephant in the room, aka Jamie, the rest of the afternoon and evening with his mom went fairly well. Giselle finally relaxed, smoothly answering every question Edna flung her way. His favorite was when she asked Giselle how old she was. Giselle winked and said, "Older than I look." His mom whispered her approval in his ear as they left. While he didn't need it, it still felt good. He knew his mother would love her.

Giselle never responded to his apology, so they drove in silence the rest of the way home. An hour later he pulled into his driveway and shut off the car. They both sat, unmoving.

"Do you still love her?" Giselle asked with a worried breath.

His Giselle was a paradox of every sort.

Sin and salvation.

Sarcasm and sincerity.

Fire and ice.

Cocky and insecure.

He had a feeling he'd be spending the rest of his life uncovering the rest of them because they ran far and deep.

Turning in his seat, he seized the back of her neck. He handled her roughly, yanking her close until his hot, angry breaths washed over her. He hoped she felt this twist deep in her gut. He hoped his rage at even that stupid-ass thought poured through her veins and scalded her like it did him.

"Fuck no, I don't still love her. I. Love. You. Giselle. Only you. It will only *ever* be you. When are you finally going to accept that what we have here is meant to be and you're all I'll ever want until my dying fucking breath? What do I have to do to make you believe that? Trust that?"

He should take her inside, pin her to the couch, and sit on her until she vomited every single insecurity that rotted her insides and crushed her belief in them. He should force her to bond with him right this fucking instant so she could never be rid of him. But instead, he unbuckled his belt and lowered the zipper on his jeans with his free hand.

"What are you doing?"

Hefting her over the console, in one angry swipe, he pushed aside the crotch of her panties, thankful she was wearing a skirt, and plunged deep in one hard cruel thrust. He hadn't even checked to see if she was ready. She wasn't.

"I'm fucking you, what does it feel like I'm doing?" His growl was a near roar. "And I'm going to fuck you every fucking minute of every fucking day until you believe every fucking word I'll ever say to you is the truth." With one hand firmly wrapped around her neck and the other bruising her hip, he pumped into her viciously. He was rougher with her than he'd ever been before, but by the way her breaths hitched and she dripped down his cock, she wasn't hating it.

"I love you, you got it?" he rumbled in her ear.

He felt her nod against his cheek but it wasn't good enough.

"The words, beautiful."

"Yes," she panted.

Already the telltale signs of her orgasm loomed. Her tight, silky walls fluttered. Her throaty moans got louder.

"You're mine forever. Say yes."

"Yes, yes."

Yeah, he had her exactly where he wanted her. Lifting the hand from her hip, he cradled her face. "We are destined mates, yes?"

Her wild, glowing eyes widened in surprise, but she never let up her pace. She was so damn close, pushing him to the brink with her.

When she nodded, he barked, "Words." He'd be damned if he'd let her leave this car without the knowledge that he *knew* she was destined to be with him and only him.

"Yes." It was only a soft puff of air, but all that mattered was she said it.

"And in the very near future, we are going to bond, Giselle. I am going to drink your blood and become yours and you will become mine."

Her body slowed; he could tell she was getting ready to protest.

"The only word that better come out of that smart mouth of yours is yes."

"Mike," she breathed. She was getting ready to rip his heart out. Fuck that. He wasn't going to let her. No way in the pits of hell was he letting this exquisite creature get away.

Tightening his grip and increasing the pace of his thrusts, he told her, "Yes, Mike, is all I want to hear right now. The rest we'll work out later. Yes, Mike. Say it."

He slinked a hand between them and started circling her hard little clit. Within seconds, she was clenching around him, but he wasn't going to let her go without some commitment first.

"Giselle," he commanded, easing his cadence, "answer me."

Her gaze focused on his. Finally, she whispered an agreeable "Yes, Mike."

Thank. Fucking. God.

"Good. Now sink those beautiful fangs into me and drink until I'm coming all over you."

She stared at him a beat before complying.

Holy God in heaven. "Giselle," he groaned harshly. *Nothing* felt as euphoric as Giselle's teeth deep in his flesh. As they both came undone in a backbiting, mind-bending climax, his stomach clenched at the thought of her essence running down his throat, pulsing through his arteries, and nourishing his soul.

He craved it. He wanted to be bound to this woman who was now sagging and spent and trembling in his arms more than the revenge that once burned within him. Now he had to make sure she honored her promise because he knew his spitfire. She'd try to come up with some lame excuse not to.

He was just waiting for it.

CHAPTER 15

Mike

He moved inside her. Slow. Steady. Their breathing got heavy. Their souls lost in each other. She tried to control the pace. He wouldn't let her. He wanted to pour every ounce of love inside him into her. Everything he was, she owned. She had it all. Even his life. Jesus, he loved her more than he thought humanly possible.

He'd woken her up this morning the way he wanted to for the next ten thousand mornings. Cock buried deep. Tongue in her mouth. Hands sweeping her lines and curves. "Now. I want to bond right now, Giselle," he whispered softly against her sweaty cheek.

She stiffened. As in, stiff as a goddamned two by four. He slowly levered on his forearms and gazed down at her terrified face. "Why are you acting like this? You agreed to this last night." He tried to keep the anger from bleeding into his tone, but he failed. Epically.

"You don't know what you're asking," she replied with such confidence it pissed him off.

"The fuck I don't," he spat. "I know *exactly* what I'm asking. I know exactly what I want, Giselle, and I've made that clear over and over, time and again that it's you. But I'm getting the distinct feeling maybe this is just one-sided."

Frustrated, he pulled away from the warmth of her body and sat on the edge of the bed, his back to her, head in his hands.

"That's not fair," she said without inflection.

On a snort, he droned, "Not fair? That's rich. I'll tell you what's not fair, Giselle." Over his shoulder, he threw words he knew would stoke her ever-burning flames into a raging inferno. "It's that you're too fucking scared to commit yourself to me for the rest of your life. That's a long fucking time to be stuck with an asshole like me, isn't it?"

Yep. That did it.

He felt the dip of the bed as she rose. "I am not scared, you fucking prick."

"Yeah?" He pushed himself up and stalked toward her. She was hastily trying to shove on her bra. He ripped it from her hands, throwing it across the room. "Then if you're not *scared*," he emphasized the taunt for good measure, "what is it, huh? My bank account too small? My house not extravagant enough? My human life too pathetic and humdrum?" Every jab drove him forward and her backward until she was pressed up between the bedroom wall and almost two hundred pounds of angry male.

"Stop it," she pleaded in a whisper.

She was close to breaking. He felt it. He just needed to push a little more. He *hated* doing this to her, but it was the only way. He had to crack her open so he could finally see inside. Flattening his palms to the wall, he pressed his still-erect shaft into her naked, vulnerable body. Her stomach quivered, but her chin went up.

He lowered his voice for maximum effect and started swinging the bat hard. "My blood not tasty enough for you? My cock not up to snuff? What's the matter, baby?" With each caustic remark he made, he felt her blood heat and her heart crack. Delivering the final blow ripped him apart. "Is one lowly human not enough to satisfy the beast in Mrs. Hyde?"

"Fuck you!" she screamed. "Fuck you, fuck you, fuck you!"

Giselle rarely used her superior strength against him, but this time, she didn't hold back. Within a blink, he found their positions reversed and *he* was the one pinned to the wall.

They'd done this the other night. After he'd stepped out of the shower, she'd pushed him against the bathroom door, dropped her robe seductively to the floor, and got herself off while giving him the best fucking blow job he'd ever had. He'd wanted to come inside her pussy, but when he'd tried pulling out of her hot little mouth, she put a hand to his stomach and easily held him there sucking until she savagely pulled the seed from his balls. It was the sexiest fucking thing he'd done.

Only now, there was no seduction. There would be no cock sucking. No moans of pleasure. The way they were going there wouldn't even be air.

With his feet barely touching the ground, her stranglehold was only increasing, cutting off his oxygen. "What's a matter?" he rasped, struggling for a lungful of life. "Hit a little too close to home, did I?"

Oh, fuck. That did it. He felt her shatter. He was afraid to look down for fear he'd see the traitorous knife in his own hand and her bloody pieces at his feet. He was a fucking asshole for doing this. If it pushed her away he'd never forgive himself.

"It's not you," she cried out. "It's not you!"

Hands on his knees, he sucked in a ragged breath—or five—when she let him go. He hated when she took a few steps back, away from him.

"It's me. Jesus," she lamented, "that's the oldest cliché known to mankind and I didn't really mean it like that. Or maybe I did." The last mumbled part nearly crushed him. He would be nothing without her. A ghost, a shell, a walking husk filled with blank space.

She flopped in the easy chair in the corner of the room and just stared at him. Long. Hard. Sad. So goddamned sad, it crushed his heart.

"I can't have children."

And there it was.

The excuse he felt coming.

Her little announcement was so emotionless, it was almost as if she was reading a headline from the Sunday paper. But he knew better. She was hurting. She really expected this revelation would end them.

Well, he had news for her. He already *knew*. Ren had some pretty enlightening info to share when they had their little bonding time and honestly, none of it made a fucking lick of anything to him, but Ren being Ren, was trying to protect Giselle. He respected that.

The vampire explained a lot of things, actually. Things Giselle would be volcanic about if she found out. Now he knew it all. Oh, not the secrets she held tight to. That overprotective vamp would never divulge those, and it wasn't his place to, but he now knew all the excuses she would use to refuse him. Every fucking one of them.

The most revealing thing Ren told him, however, was just because he was her one and only didn't mean he had to bond with her. He could say fuck it and walk. What no one seemed to get was he *couldn't*. He wouldn't.

"Then we'll adopt, if that's what you want."

"Just like that?"

"Just like what, Giselle?" He slowly ate up the gap they had between them and knelt at her feet. "Listen, *really* listen to what I've been telling you. About how much I love you. About how nothing else about you matters than what I see right before me."

When water glassed her eyes and began streaming in little zigzag rivers down her face, he felt flayed, but continued on. They needed to do this. Old scabs needed to be reopened so he could sew them shut his way. Not with Steri-Strips, but real fucking stitches that took the wound with it when they finally dissolved.

He looked up into her forlorn eyes and laid it all on the line. "I know a lot of things you think I don't. I understand that vampires bond only with their human Moiras, their Fated mates and that I am your Fated. That to bond we exchange blood during sex. I'll grow fangs. I'll inherit your speed and strength, stamina, and skills. I'll stop aging. I'll be sustained by your blood and you by mine. My longevity is tied singularly to yours. As long as you live, so do I. You die, I die. But I die, and you die as well. I also know female vampires can't bear children. I know all of this, Giselle, and I still choose us, because without you I'm a dead man walking anyway. I was lifeless before you came along and I will be again if you leave me."

Giselle's hand now covered her mouth, stifling her sobs. "How...how do you know all this?"

"Well," he said gruffly while pushing to his feet. Lifting Giselle, he settled her on his lap. He literally sighed with relief when she melted into him and laid her head on his shoulder. This right here was perfection. "Let's just say I have an informant on the inside."

"Who?"

"Sorry. Guy code." He lightly stroked her pale thigh. It felt like finely spun silk under the pads of his fingers. Against his will, he was growing hard again.

"Ren," she said flatly.

When he didn't reply, she tilted her head and captured his eyes. He was sap because all he could think to himself was he'd always be her willing captive. "It was him, wasn't it?"

"If that's what you think you'll have to ask him yourself."

"I have ways of making humans spill." To prove her

point she squirmed against his erection, making him moan. Oh, the irony. It took him months to get her in his bed and now he could hardly get them out of it. And not that he was against it, but continual fucking didn't allow for a lot of talking. And they needed to talk.

"Giselle," he groaned in denied agony. "I want you on my cock more than anything, but we need to talk."

"Sounds serious," she whispered against his lips before giving him a soul-searching kiss. She didn't have to search for it because it was already hers.

"I'm going to see Jamie."

She froze, easing away slowly. Before she could get too far, he clamped down, holding her to him.

"Before you freak out, it's not what you're thinking. I need to close this chapter in my life. For me. For *us*. Our pasts can never be erased, but I do think the slate can be wiped somewhat clean. Once the ink has touched that whiteboard, it will always linger, but it also fades until it becomes almost indistinguishable. So I choose to move ahead with you with a clean, ink-free slate. That is...if you'll have me?"

The corner of her mouth tried to kick up. "I will. I do...I just..." She takes in a deep, thoughtful breath and looks down at her lap as if she's afraid to say the next part while looking at him. "Can I just have a little time?"

He didn't like that idea. The more time she put between them, the easier it would be for her to keep pushing them along, never committing, never purging, never really living. But if she needed it he'd give her a little rope. About half an inch is all. "Okay. How much time do you need?"

Sweeping her gaze back to his, she said, "I don't know really. I...I have something in my past I need to take care of, too."

He didn't like the strange buzz he was getting from her. She was keeping something from him, and he had a goddamned good idea what it was. He also knew the vampire who cared for her like a sister was trying to erase Giselle's board once and for all, unbeknownst to her. Ren was a good ally, a good male, and a good friend to Giselle—one he now had immeasurable respect for.

"You really don't care about the baby thing?"

Cupping her cheek, he made sure she was looking straight into his eyes when he told her, "No. I don't care. All I need is you, Giselle. But if somehow in the future we're presented with a chance to become parents and it's what we want, then we shouldn't close our minds to it."

She nodded absently.

"What else you got?"

Her curved brows furrowed. "What does that mean?"

"It means what other excuses for not bonding are you gonna throw at me? Because I'm ready, so fucking bring them all on. Right now, so we can get them out of the way. I don't want to have this conversation again."

"They're not excuses, Mike. They're real issues."

"Perception isn't reality, baby."

"Mike," she blew with exasperation.

"Giselle," he piped back.

Picking her up, he repositioned her over his stiff shaft and let her sink down. She was so damn wet, she took his size with ease. They fit together like yin and yang.

"Fuck, you feel good. Any other excuses you want to discuss?" he asked, thumbing her distended nipples. Rolling them between his forefinger and thumb, he got them nice and big before he closed his mouth around one.

"No," she moaned, arching into him.

"Good. Tell me, baby, when we're bonded will I be able to fuck you for days on end without my cock falling off?" Dragging his tongue along her goose-pebbled flesh, he made his way to the other nub. He could tell it felt neglected.

When she laughed, it made her core tighten and the

earlier release he'd been denied reared its head all too damn soon. "Yes."

"Then don't take too long. I'm not very patient, you know."

Swiveling her hips, she held onto his shoulders for leverage. Then, using the strength in her thighs, she started riding him hard as he sucked the favorite spot on her neck. "I thought you said you were a patient man when you wanted something bad enough."

"I lied. I'm not fucking patient at all," he panted against her.

"Well, you'll have a lot of time to learn that particular skill."

Tangling his fist in her hair, he pulled her down for a toe-curling kiss. His balls were so tight and drawn they screamed. He needed a release, but not before her. He practically tossed Giselle off him and with her hands now braced on his dresser and their gazes locked in the mirror, he drove back into her soaked channel so hard her feet lifted from the ground.

"Will I, now?" he grunted.

"Yes. Yes, you will." She could hardly speak. He could barely think.

"God, I fucking love you." Knotting his hand through her golden locks once again, he pulled until her back was bowed and her mouth met his.

"You do have a way with words, Detective," she mumbled.

"And with my cock."

"And with your cock. Always with your cock," she admitted. A light laugh morphed into a gasp right before she cried his name and fell, taking him with her. When they'd ridden out every ounce of their orgasms together, he let his body blanket hers. Wrapping his arms around her, Mike planted a series of gentle kisses along her shoulder blades while he regained his senses.

They were so damn close to the top of the stairs

they'd been climbing for months now. So close to opening that next door and stepping through. But they had a few more steps to go. These would be toughest and steepest of them all.

They both still had history to face, a yoke to sever. And letting your past go was never as easy as it sounded.

CHAPTER 16

REN

Looking around, one would deduce they'd stumbled into a crack house, but they'd be wrong. The place Siobhan would meet his demise was a small below-ground room in an exclusive Miami sex club in Key Biscayne, an affluent part of the city.

The gloomy, humid, windowless room stunk of piss, lost innocence, and shattered dreams. Stains of virtue, discarded condom wrappers, and used needles littered the fissured concrete floor. Mold grew in the cracks of the limestone walls, which held pleas of mercy and screams of terror. The corners were peppered with dried-up shells of insects caught in a different sort of web, one that had the same lethal edge as the young females who were tortured and defiled here. He wondered how many ghosts haunted this place, their souls trapped in perpetual torment from how violently they'd left this Earth.

Getting into this club hadn't been easy. Siobhan was a paranoid bastard and had this place spelled so no vamps could flash in and out—a trick Xavier had also used. Little did he know they also now had a witch in their pocket. It was no secret Damian and Giselle weren't on the best of terms, so it took a lot of convincing and downright begging, but Ren finally got Damian to allow Analise to help them bypass the witchery so they could enter undetected. Against her wishes, Damian then sent her home while he waited for his part in this little setup.

Siobhan was slippery, moving constantly, rarely staying in a community more than a few weeks. The only thing that had kept him alive all these years was he *never* returned to the same place. But they'd orchestrated a very special treat for him he wouldn't be able to pass up. And that single error in judgment would cost him his life.

Apparently Siobhan had a "type." He liked them with fire and fight; he didn't do broken ones. The younger the better. Stark blonde, alabaster skin, piercing blue eyes. Eerily like Elle, which was exactly how they'd lured him here tonight. With a Giselle replica.

After all this time, after all the chasing and frustration, tonight was *his* night. Ren would eliminate this tainted waste of cells and blood and space, doing both vampires and humankind a service, a kindness. Because tonight they had a secret weapon they didn't have before.

Fucking Geoffrey.

Ren couldn't believe his luck. Geoffrey, a once-rogue vampire turned ally, was going to be the key to taking this depraved piece of shit out. Geoffrey's skill of mimicry had recently saved the all-powerful Romaric's ass, as well as that of his brother, Taiven, and tonight, Geoffrey would be the bait that lured a monster to his own fiery wedge of hell.

A shiver of anticipation ran up his spine and settled in the form of a wicked grin on his face. He cracked his knuckles and rolled his neck around on his shoulders a couple of times to loosen his tense muscles.

The weak, muffled cries of a young girl in the distance alerted him it was showtime. The "girl" would be brought in by her human handler. Ren would love nothing more than to slit his throat and let him bleed out nice and slow, but then the absence of the handler outside the door and the scent of blood would alert Siobhan something was off. He was already skittish; then they'd lose their one chance. So the human was getting a gift, really. He'd live, at least for now. Then, after they were done dispatching Siobhan, he'd carve the fucker up like a Thanksgiving turkey.

The sound of metal clanging against metal and the twist of a key in the door signaled go-time. Per the plan, Ren flashed into the empty room next door and waited. When he heard the grate of heavy alloy against concrete and the snick of the lock being engaged, he reentered.

According to their source, they had about three minutes until Siobhan arrived. After that, things would move quickly. He wished he could take his time, making the motherfucker suffer the way he'd made Elle and so many others suffer, but time was not a luxury they had. So the kill would be swift and sure.

"Nice of you to join the party," a low female voice rasped.

Christ almighty, knowing this was Geoffrey but hearing an entirely different voice come out of a tiny, almost nude, beat-up female body was fucking unnerving. And leaving her (him) like this, uncovered and vulnerable, went against his every protective instinct.

"You thought I was gonna leave you for dead, didn't you?" he chuckled lightly forcing his eyes away. They kept their voices low to avoid attracting attention. Even though the rooms were supposedly soundproofed, he wasn't taking any chances.

"The thought did cross my mind."

"Yeah?" he asked, preparing to lean his bulk against the wall, when he thought better of it and straightened.

"We aren't exactly BFFs," Geoffrey drawled.

Ren regarded him for a few moments, trying hard to see through the broken façade to the vampire inside. This was the third time Geoffrey had put his own life at risk for the Lords.

The first was when he battled Xavier and almost bit it with an actual gutting—as in they had to pick his innards from the floor and carry them home.

The second was when he willingly offered his services to Rom, ending Rom's tyrannical father.

And now. When Ren approached him, Geoffrey jumped on board, no hesitation. He hadn't explained the details, really, because that wasn't any of his business. Just said this was retribution for a past wrong. Explained what this SOB had been doing to young females and he agreed on the spot. In addition to being cunning, Siobhan was a mighty powerful vamp. He could easily end them. Geoffrey was genuinely putting his life at risk here. And for what? Because he was simply asked? It seemed so. There was definitely more to this rogue than met the eye.

"Eh, you're growing on me," he bounced back easily. "You ready?"

"Was fucking born ready, vampire." The surety and command of his voice belied the position Geoffrey now found himself in.

Geoffrey's female form knelt on the hard floor, legs bound apart by a spreader attached to both her feet and her upper thighs. Her arms were stretched overhead, shackled to a rusty metal ring drilled in the wall. There was a thick black collar around her neck and clipped to it was a nice heavy chain running the length of her back that the male violating her could use as a leash and then as a murder weapon when he was finished. This helpless, young, beaten, and bruised female had been reduced to nothing more than a sacrificial fucking lamb for the malevolent beast sent in to devour her.

It was stomach churning to think about the countless females who had really been in this position. It was heartbreaking to know Elle had been one of them.

Knowing it was almost showtime, Ren fanned out his senses again. The three floors above crawled with humans. There were also six vamps on the premises, but that was just sheer coincidence. Siobhan would come with his own security detail. If he kept true to pattern, he'd arrive with just two bodyguards, both of whom would remain upstairs while he took his time with his victim. That's where Damian came in. Keep them nice and distracted while they made their kill.

Suddenly three new auras appeared.

They pulsed with power and corruption and greed.

Bingo.

They were here.

"It's time, rogue. Try to stay alive."

"I didn't live through twenty kinds of hell to die now. You just do your job and leave me to mine," Geoffrey chided.

Ren barked a short laugh. "See ya on the flip side." He flashed back to the other room and the waiting game began. This was the hardest part. He wanted to slaughter, to burn, to destroy. He wanted to slice that depraved motherfucker's head off the second he walked through the door, but battle required strategy and infinite patience or else it was your head that ended up meeting the ground instead of your enemy's.

This was also the riskiest part for Geoffrey. Ren still couldn't believe he'd agreed to go through with it. But to maintain the element of surprise, they had to catch Siobhan at his most vulnerable, which meant... Well, let's just say Ren had a whole new level of respect for the rogue. This was not his fight, yet the vampire proved selfless once again, literally taking one for the team.

The minutes ticked by like hours. Siobhan had

entered a short while ago after a brief exchange with the handler, whom he sent on his way, leaving only the three of them on this level.

Ren didn't know what to expect, but pillow talk certainly wasn't it. The degenerate praised Geoffrey on her body, her looks, her "sweet, pink, hairless cunt." Mother. Fucker. His fingers itched to kill. His blood thrummed for vengeance. His patience was a hair trigger away from splintering. But he had to hold until the precise moment—he was only getting one shot at this. He would not let impatience fuck it up.

Geoffrey's performance was Oscar worthy. He whimpered and cried out, pitching his voice high, pleading for mercy he'd never be granted. The sharp tang of blood wafted through the walls, making his incisors involuntarily drop.

When Geoffrey finally uttered their predetermined string of code words, "Enjoy your dance with the devil, motherfucker," Ren palmed his favored katana and flashed right behind Siobhan. His sword was already halfway to its target before he'd even taken solid form.

The bastard never saw it coming, had no time to react. Pants dropped to his ankles and bent over a restrained, defenseless animate body, Ren took immense pleasure swiftly separating Siobhan's head from his shoulders, where it dropped to the floor with a sick, resounding thud.

It was done.

Finished.

The finality of revenge was complete.

After spending one hundred twenty years as a goddamned ghost, Siobhan's face would forever be twisted halfway between divine pleasure and pure shock.

A fitting end, he thought.

The entire thing took half a second at most, but he would always recall the sound of metal splitting the air in half. He'd forever feel the first contact of the razor-sharp blade before it smoothly sliced flesh and cartilage and bone. The smell of retribution would live eternally within him.

Ren stood motionless, soaking in the scent of bittersweet victory. Hot, thick vengeance coated his face, his clothes, his shoes. It dripped from the tip of tempered steel, forming a growing pool at his feet where the rest of Siobhan's limp body lay twitching, not quite realizing he wasn't violating an innocent anymore.

"You okay?" Ren asked Geoffrey absently.

"Fucking divine," he replied curtly, back to himself. He stood naked as a jaybird, splattered with blood. "How the hell do you think I am after that sick fuck had his hands and his dick all over me? Depraved motherfucker." Geoffrey's foot connected with Siobhan's now lifeless corpse so hard it bounced off the opposite wall and sprayed them both with a fresh gore of triumph.

"Feel better?"

"Fuck no. I'll need to take the first couple layers of skin off before his evil stench will be erased. Light him up. We're out of time."

Geoffrey was right. The bodyguards would be here any second if Damian's attempt to divert their attention didn't work.

Ren dipped his hand into his pocket and withdrew an antique silver-plated lighter that belonged to his pappi. The front displayed a curvy, nude goddess intricately carved from ivory. One of the very first lighters ever made, it was probably worth a mint but was priceless to him. Turning it over in his hand once, he flicked the striker.

Nothing happened.

Again.

Once again...nada.

"You fucking with me right now?" Geoffrey said, his voice grating as he paced nervously. "Cuz if you are, I gotta say I don't like your brand of humor much."

Sending up a quick prayer to his pappi, he struck a third time. Glorious flames erupted from the old flint tube. Ren threw Geoffrey a smirk before striding over to the prone empty shell of a vamp. Bending down, he held the fire to Siobhan's expensive linen pants, watching with glee as they caught. The blaze spread quickly, engulfing him entirely within a matter of seconds. Making his way across the small room, Ren kicked Siobhan's severed head toward the orange glow, morbidly hypnotized as it rolled lopsidedly away from him toward the fire.

"This place is going to go up like dry timber," Geoffrey announced, glancing at the wood beams above their heads.

"Yep," Ren replied flatly. This club had housed depraved activities for God knows how long. Tonight, it would be burned to the ground, right along with this dead vamp. Ren knew another would pop up in its place like a fucking weed, but at least, he could rest easy tonight knowing *this* one was toast. Literally.

"I'm not going to be responsible for any more innocent lives," Geoffrey challenged.

"Got it covered." He may want this place gone, but he didn't want innocents trapped in the crosshairs either, even though evil walked unknowingly among them. So he caught a pretty little redhead on her way inside earlier and *persuaded* her to pull the fire alarm...just...about...now.

As if on cue, the blare of shrill bells echoed around them, signaling it was time to go.

Right before he gave Geoffrey the nod to make their leave, Ren noticed a thick pendant lying in a red river of justice a few feet away. Knowing exactly what he needed to do with it, he quickly scooped it up.

"Souvenir?" Geoffrey inquired snidely, eyes flitting between the medallion and his face.

More like a bolt cutter, so Giselle could cleave the past once and for all.

"Yeah," he said, taking one last glance at the vamp burning to ash. "Something like that."

CHAPTER 17

Giselle

"No, no, like this. You have to support the neck."
Kate stood next to Giselle with the tiniest being she'd
ever seen, wrapped up like a taco in a white blanket with
yellow ducks all over it. She started backing away, but
Kate kept coming at her.

It had been two weeks since the raid on Xavier.
Giselle knew they'd rescued a number of children,
but she had no idea how many women and kids
were brought here to the shelter. Mainly because she
didn't care. And it's not that she was as soulless as
everyone thought. It was that there was nothing she
could offer.

Even though she had firsthand understanding of
what these abused females had been through, she wasn't
about to swap stories in some little group therapy
session she'd heard Kate led. No fucking way. Her pain
was hers and hers alone, and sharing it didn't ease it. It
was reliving it.

And Giselle absolutely wasn't the lovey-dovey
motherly type these kids needed. She wasn't full of
warmth or comfort or soft words. She was limited on

affection and definitely short on love. Who in their right mind would want her poisoning an unsullied child?

Up until this morning, Dev had not once suggested she come here and "help out." So why she was now standing in a small nursery in the shelter was a puzzle she was still trying to work. This stank of Ren, actually. If she found out he was behind this, she'd cut his nutsack open before she sliced his dick off and fed him cock and balls for dinner.

"I think this is all a mistake. Dev must have been delirious when he asked me to come help you. I don't do babies. Maybe he thought you were working with the women today, not"—she waved—"these."

And he hadn't really *asked*. Dev didn't ask. He demanded. She'd tried to protest because Mike was talking to Jamie today and, selfishly, she wanted to be there when he was done. But you didn't say no to the Midwest Regent Vampire Lord. So here she was.

"No, he knew what I was doing today," she replied with some amusement.

"Do you find this funny?" Giselle spat angrily. She may have apologized to Dev's mate the other night, but she wasn't going to make a fucking habit of it. If Kate did something to piss her off, she'd let her bitch off the leash.

Kate started laughing, which startled the baby, making him howl. Giselle took another step back. With ease, Kate propped him up against her chest and started patting him lightly on the back as she cooed in his ear. He quieted instantly.

"You should see the look on your face right now," Kate said, chuckling as she bounced the little one back and forth.

"And what look is that," Giselle retorted, a little fascinated at how natural Kate was with handling an infant. She reluctantly admitted Kate would make a good mother. A very good one, actually. As upset as

Giselle had been the other day about never being able to have children, she had to confess in her case maybe that unknown power knew best. And now that Mike was okay with not having children, she'd actually put the thought behind her entirely.

"A cross between petrified and unglued."

"That's not true." It was. Bitch.

Kate shrugged. "Okay. Whatever you say. Here." With a hand behind the baby's neck and one under its butt, she held the bundle out to her. "Take her."

Her heart stuttered a couple of beats.

Her?

A female vampire?

"Her?" Giselle parroted in shock. Female vampires were few and far between and she knew it was Xavier's vile pleasure to destroy them if born within his walls. She couldn't believe this little female had beaten unimaginable odds and made it out alive. What would become of her?

"Yes, *her*. Take her. I have two more I need to feed and we're short-staffed and she's been very fussy today."

"Well...what am I supposed to do with her?" she asked with genuine confusion.

Kate nodded to the rocker in the corner of the nursery. "She's been fed and changed, so just hold her. Rock her. Sing to her." She paused. Giselle could tell she wanted to say something else, but she hedged.

"What? Just spit it out already."

Kate's lips thinned. "Maybe love her a little. I think that's what she needs. All of the kids seem attention starved, but the babies are the worst. I doubt they've had a chance to bond with anyone."

Ah. So that's why she hesitated. Giselle couldn't give love, affection. Was that it? Well, fuck her. She'd show Kate just how fucking affectionate she could be. She managed with Mike okay. How hard can something that doesn't even weigh ten pounds and can't talk back be, really?

She reached out and took the baby tentatively into her own arms, holding her the way she'd seen Kate do. She was surprisingly light. And wiggly.

"You're not going to break her." Kate adjusted her hold slightly and stood back, looking a little nervous. She had a right to be. Giselle didn't know fuck all about kids. She had to wonder why the hell Dev sent her over here in the first place.

Uncomfortable with the way Kate was examining her, she huffed, "Just go...do whatever else it is you need to. I got this."

"You're sure?"

"You need help, right?" she snapped.

Kate's head bobbed up and down. "Yes."

"Then go. I'm sure I can find you if I need to. But don't worry," she added quickly, "I won't need to. I'll be fine. *We'll* be fine."

"Okay. Thanks," Kate said tentatively. "She might need to be burped again. Just hold her up on your shoulder like I did and gently pat her back." After the last instruction, Kate made her way toward the door as Giselle sat in the chair and started pushing them back and forth. Just then she realized something.

"Kate," she called.

Kate stopped and turned. "Yeah?"

"What's her name?"

One shoulder lifted and dropped. "I don't know. We've just numbered all the babies and younger ones who can't talk yet. The older ones know their names. She's number one."

What the fuck? They've *numbered* them? She may be cold, but damn...that just seemed heartless.

"You mean she doesn't have a name?" she asked, incensed.

"No. We thought her new parents should name her."

She had new parents already? Why did that thought make her stomach drop and her chest hurt? And where the hell were they? *Who* were they? Were they loving or would they abuse their power? Would they accept a rare female into their family and love her like their own flesh and blood? Give her everything her little heart desired? Treat her like a princess but raise her like a warrior? Had they been vetted? Was there even such thing as vampire adoption? Was that what they planned to do? Adopt them all out like strays from the pound?

"Why aren't they here then?"

"Who?"

"Her new parents? Where are they?"

Kate smiled sadly. "We haven't found them yet. We're just trying to get our arms around the mess we have first and then figure out how we find new homes for them. We've DNA matched two of the young ones and one of the teenagers with their rescued mothers, but we still have over a dozen ranging from five weeks to fifteen years to find families for and we're not exactly sure how to go about that yet. It's not like there's a vampire adoption playbook we're following here."

Giselle thought on that a few beats.

"So it could be months before you find her a new family?"

"I suppose so."

Months. This little precious thing could go weeks and weeks without a mother or father. She was familyless...just as Giselle had been. Another ache built. It made her sick to ask, but she had to. "What was done to them? To the kids?" *To number one*?

"We don't know for sure," Kate responded, sighing quietly. "That will certainly be a complication when trying to find families to take them. We're just taking things one day at a time right now. It's one monumental clusterfuck, that's for sure."

Giselle smiled at that. She didn't hear Kate swear often. "You can say that again."

"Trust me, I've said it so often these past few days I think the kids are starting to parrot it. So...you okay then?" Her gaze flicked to the baby girl in Giselle's arms, then back to Giselle. Number one made a noise that was pretty close to a cry, so Giselle shook her gently. The baby quieted. She breathed an internal a sigh of relief, keeping her outer self cool, calm, and collected. Feigned as if this was a walk in the park when it felt like a walk over hot burning coals instead.

"I'm good."

"Holler if you need anything."

"I won't. Need anything, that is." Even if she did, she'd figure it out on her own. Surprisingly, she wanted Kate to have faith in her. Even more surprisingly, she wanted to prove to herself she could do this.

Kate had disappeared, leaving the two of them alone but reappeared almost immediately back in the doorway.

"Wow, that was fast. Think I'd drop her on her head already or something?" Giselle asked with a whole heap of sarcasm.

Kate's smile took up her whole face. "No. I was just going to say I think this is the longest civil conversation we've ever had."

The side of Giselle's mouth tried to turn up but she forced it flat. "I think maybe you're right."

"I liked it. Thanks for your help, Giselle."

And before Giselle could even formulate a sarcastic reply, Kate was gone again. This time, she clicked the door closed so they were shut out from the commotion of the shelter.

Well shit. Now, Kate probably thought they were "friends" or something, just as Sarah did. Next time Giselle saw Kate, she would bet everything she owned she'd try to pick back up where they left off like long-lost buds. And pretty soon, word would get out and Queen number three would be in on the action, and she'd have to start shopping and going to book club and learning how to paint toenails. Jesus Christ, if this is what being nice to one of the Lord's mates entailed, she was going to frost the hell back up.

Number one made another noise, but this time, it sounded something like a squeaky coo. Giselle hadn't even really looked at the baby yet. It was hard to see anything through the enchilada she was stuffed in.

Her head slowly fell downward when the feeling hit. It shimmered in the air right before it happened. Just as when she first set eyes on her detective, her Fated, she knew her life was about to take yet another uncontrolled turn.

When her gaze latched onto the tiny, innocent life she held a little too tightly to her chest she immediately knew she was right. Sparkling emerald eyes stared back at her, snaring her. Completely enthralling her. In the blink of an eye, her entire world didn't just shift on its axis...it fell off.

Her heart swelled.

Her insides flooded from the rapid ice melt this beautiful baby triggered.

Her purpose in life was finally defined.

Had someone told her a few months ago that after one hundred and forty years alone, she would have found not one, but two beings she would fall hopelessly in love with, she would have laughed in their face before throat punching them.

Yet here she was.

Totally, hopelessly, irrevocably, instantly in love with baby number one.

Number one cooed again and Giselle could swear she smiled at her. And that was it. She was done. Bought and wrapped with a simple, innocent gesture that was probably only caused by a gas bubble. But she didn't care.

She didn't care what chemicals floated in her tiny body. She didn't care how she came into being. She didn't care she wasn't mother material. She didn't care she wasn't bonded yet and she hadn't even thought about discussing her decision with her Fated first. She didn't care about a damn thing but this little innocent baby that she was calling dibs on.

Come hell or high water, number one was hers.

CHAPTER 18

Mike

Mike ran his palms down his denims, leaving clammy sweat behind. He wasn't ready for this. Wasn't sure he ever would be. Nerves ate a hole in his gut, but this was the right thing to do. After his last conversation with Jamie, he wasn't even sure she'd see him. She'd said memories of him had helped her make it through her darkest days but it was hard to look at him because he also reminded her of that place and those monsters. Slicing the skin from his flesh would have hurt less.

But like the glutton he was, he was back for more. This time, though, it was for him. Not her. That felt selfish, yet he'd spent so many damn years thinking only of Jamie and his revenge in her name he couldn't drum up enough guilt to talk himself out of this.

He knew coming here today that Jamie had agreed to see him. He was just hoping Giselle would be waiting at the end of it, wrapping him in her arms once again if he needed it. But Dev sent her to the shelter to help Kate, instead, leaving him here on his own.

Dev wasn't a bad guy. Not really. He'd always treated Mike with respect and fairness even when Mike had treated him like a shitbag.

And now he was helping him once again.

Mike heard footsteps. His eyes swept from the floor to the doorway expecting to see Jamie standing there. It wasn't. It was Dev.

"She's not coming, is she?" he asked dejectedly.

"She is. She'll be just a few minutes. I thought maybe you'd like some coffee while you wait."

His eyes narrowed. "Uh, sure. Don't you, ah, have servants for that?"

Chuckling, Dev walked to the chair across from him and sat. "I do. Hooker will be in shortly with it. Black, right?"

"Right," he replied, surprised that the Vampire Lord would remember how he took his coffee. He was their "guest" for a while several months back, but honestly, he didn't think anyone had paid a lick of attention to him. "Thanks."

Mike eased back against the plush cushions of his own chair, staring at the powerhouse across from him. Suddenly a thought took hold and before he could push it through the right filter, he was blurting, "Is there anyone I need ask permission from to bond with Giselle?"

Yeah. He was a fucking idiot.

If the vamp was surprised, he didn't show it. Dev leaned forward, elbows on his knees. The move stretched his button-down tight across his biceps and chest, leaving no doubt what the vampire packed underneath his innocuous-looking attire. Pure, lethal power. "Are you seeking my permission, human?"

Fuck. He should have just kept his mouth shut, shut, shut, but he didn't want to pussy out now. He wished he'd waited and asked Ren what the right protocol was instead.

"Is it your permission I should be asking for?"

At that moment, Hooker breezed into the library, handing him a piping mug of coffee. He took a tentative sip and just about moaned. Jesus, these vamps must have magic coffee beans or something.

With a grace that defied such raw power, Dev eased back and threw one leg over the other. "And what if I said no."

His answer was immediate. "Then I guess I'd tell you I didn't fucking care. I'm going to bond with her anyway."

The Vampire Lord's smile was slow and practically predatory. "Well, that's not really how it works in our world anyway. As long as Giselle wants you, that's all that's relevant."

Mike nodded once; glad this train wreck discussion was over.

"Are you okay with all this? Becoming a *bloodsucker*?" The dig was said in humor, but he heard Dev's underlying concern. It was the same tone Ren had.

"Surprisingly enough, I am. Each day I go without that bond, an ache grows. It's...hard to explain." Let alone understand.

"Oh, I understand perfectly," Dev snorted in agreement.

Taking another sip of his coffee, Mike contemplated how much his world was about to change. He wouldn't need much sleep, not that he got much anyway. He wouldn't be as powerful as a full-blooded vampire, but he'd be pretty damn close. But what did all this mean for him? What would he do all day? Year after year? Just be the Vampire Lord's gopher? He didn't want that. He needed a purpose. A real one.

"I'd like a permanent position on your staff."

"You already have one," Dev replied coolly.

"I'm not talking about your errand boy. I'm talking about a real contribution."

"Doing?"

"I don't know. I haven't thought it all the way through, but even you have to admit my skills are valuable. I have contacts all over the country. Maybe I could track down the biological families of the kids you rescued or something along those lines?"

Hell, he'd done it before with Sarah's family, and the feeling of accomplishment was a high he'd only ridden when he closed a cold case. Or when he was balls deep inside of Giselle. But he couldn't make a full-time job out of that.

Could he?

Dev looked impressed as he nodded slowly. "I think that's something we could discuss."

"Good."

"Good."

"I'm not going to call you my lord," Mike quipped, taking another sip of the gold in his cup.

Dev rose with ease. "Never expected anything less from you, human."

Mike's quick rebuttal about not being human for long held fast to his tongue when he looked over and saw Jamie standing in the doorway watching them. He practically tripped over himself standing, spilling his hot drink in the process.

"Hi," he said quietly. He wiped his wet hand off on his jeans before setting the mug down.

"Hi," she replied just as softly.

"Well, that's my cue. We'll talk about this topic later." Dev's voice echoed somewhere to his left.

"Thanks," he mumbled, not even aware of Dev's exit. "Do you, ah, do you want to sit down?" He gestured to the chair Dev just vacated. Jamie shyly made her way to it. The breadth of the furniture swallowed her delicate frame and all he could do was stare at the woman he once thought he would marry.

Jesus, she was breathtaking. She looked so different than the last time he laid eyes on her. Her brown hair was shinier, a little shorter and had hints of red in it now. She'd gone blonde back in college, but he liked her natural brown so much better. Her pale skin had life to it again. Her stick figure had filled out substantially. But the thing that stunned him the most was the haunted look that weighed down her soul was nearly gone.

She looked almost...normal.

She looked beautiful.

"Wow. You look great," he said on a pained breath.

Her smile was genuine. "Thanks. I'm feeling...much better."

"I'm glad. Truly."

Several awkward heartbeats went by before either of them said anything. Then they both spoke at once.

"Have you—"

"How are—"

Her light, lyrical laugh brought back hordes of memories. Swarms of them buzzed around his head until his ears rang.

Their first kiss.

The morning of her eighteenth birthday when he gave her a pair of diamond chip studs he'd saved months for.

How he felt like he'd puke when he told her he loved her for the first time.

The night he took her virginity.

Minutes that dragged on like centuries after she went missing.

The self-flagellation he'd done every fucking day since then.

Drunken nights and countless women he'd drowned in trying to numb himself.

Despair. Hatred. Helplessness.

For the first time, he thought maybe he understood how she felt last time they'd met. Good and bad all wrapped up into one warped, bastardized package. When he looked at her now, that's what he saw. Blissful and cruel memories twined together until they became an indistinguishable blob of heartbreak.

"You go first," she said with another smile.

He swallowed hard, wondering where he should start. Wondering what this was really going to accomplish. "I heard your little sister is getting married," he told her. He had no idea if she'd kept up on any outside news, but he wanted her to know. She was marrying a big-time lawyer who was quite the shits in Minneapolis. So big, in fact, their engagement earned a thirty-second spot on the nightly news all the way in Milwaukee.

"Yeah, I saw that, too. She looks happy."

"You think maybe you'll go?"

Looking away, she replied quietly, "No."

He felt incredibly sad that Jamie wouldn't be able to do all the things sisters did together when one of them got married. Showers, wedding dress shopping, bachelorette parties. Even though six years separated them, he knew how close Jamie and Jackie were. He'd envied their relationship, actually, not having any siblings of his own.

"You haven't contacted your parents yet, then?"

Her face fell. His stomach went with it. He never wanted another ounce of sadness for her. "No. I'm not sure..." Her eyes narrowed. "I'm not sure that will ever be a good idea. I'm not the daughter they lost. I'll never be her again."

His mouth turned down. She was right. Jamie was the all-American girl with her entire future ahead of her. She was studying premed and had aspirations to become a world-class cardiothoracic surgeon. She was brilliant, likable, and driven. He wondered how much of her still lingered.

"Maybe you'll change your mind someday?"

Thoughtful for a few moments, she finally said, "I don't think so."

Not wanting silence to fill the space between them, he asked dumbly, "You been sleeping okay?"

She guffawed. "That still eludes me most nights."

"Don't they have something they can give you that will help?" He hated the thought she was still scared to close her eyes.

One shoulder shrugged. "They do, but I just can't stomach the thought of taking anything foreign inside my body again if I can absolutely avoid it."

He still didn't know any details about what happened in her years of captivity. He thought he wanted to at one point, but he wasn't so sure anymore. "Oh fuck, Jamie. I'm sorry. That was a stupid thing to say."

"No, it wasn't. And please don't be sorry, Mike."

He should leave. What the hell did he think he was accomplishing by dredging this shit up? "I should go," he said in resignation.

"No, don't." Her reply was quick and assured.

"Jamie..." He let her name linger and was drawn into eyes that used to remind him of melted caramel. He hadn't eaten a fucking caramel since the day his old life died and his new one started. "You sure?"

"Very." The turn of her lips reached her eyes. If it hadn't, he'd be gone.

"Okay then. Ah, tell me what you've been doing with your time here." It had been six months since Jamie was rescued, and as far as he knew she hadn't even left the palatial estate.

Jamie regarded him for a few moments before she launched into a description of her daily routine. One-on-one counseling, group counseling, meditation, visualization. Apparently someone on Dev's staff had been teaching self-defense classes, so she recently started taking those. She'd taken to helping in the kitchen and was trying to learn the art of pastry making. She said she'd been reading a bit, which was something he remembered she used to have a passion for. And she'd become pretty good friends with one of the other long-term residents at the shelter named Chelsea.

She was animated, talking with her hands the way he

remembered. The longer she spoke, the more hints of the old Jamie shone through. God. He never expected this in a hundred years. He wasn't sure how he thought she'd be, but a mile down the road to recovery wasn't it.

"So, now that I've answered your twenty questions, you get to answer one of mine," she said pointedly. "What are you really doing here?"

He couldn't help but smile. One of the things he'd loved most about her was her directness. She was nothing like Giselle, not even on the same playing field. Jamie's tenacity, though, like Giselle's, had been a draw for him.

But his smile faded pretty fucking fast when the real reason he was here crossed his mind. *Because I'm going to bond with a vampire, turning into the very thing that destroyed you.*

Fuck.

Fuuuuck.

This was a horribly, epically bad idea.

The guilt he already carried about Jamie sat on him like a metric ton and telling her the real reason may very well set her back. He couldn't have that on his conscience. He shouldn't have come.

Ready to tell her he'd made a mistake, he froze when she reached across the space that separated them and touched her fingertips to his. Just barely. Right on the ends. They were baby smooth and cool.

He looked down, staring at how small and fine her fingers were compared to his. He wondered how many tears she'd cried into them over the eleven years she was gone. How many pleas were absorbed, never to be answered. His eyes pricked. Before he knew it his thumb unconsciously started rubbing the flesh just above her nails.

"I just want you to be okay," he whispered brokenly, still staring at their hands. A heaviness sat in the middle of his chest. He wondered if it would ever go away. "I need to know you'll be okay, Jamie. You need to be okay." The last plea barely had sound.

He heard her inhale deeply and blow it out slowly. Then she was on the floor in front of him, looking up at him. Looking into him. She had a slight curve to her lips, but he wouldn't call it a smile exactly. It was more like acceptance. A reluctant acknowledgment for the shit circumstances life dealt them both.

"I need you to do the same thing, Mike. I need to know that *you'll* be okay and not carry guilt that's not yours to bear."

"But—"

"No, Mike," she interrupted. "There is no *but*. There is no *what-if*. There is no *I wish*. Thinking that way is sheer mental and emotional torture and doesn't do a damn thing to change the circumstances. You don't think I've said the same thing to myself day after day for the last eleven years? What if I'd let you take me out that night like you'd wanted to? What if I'd had one less drink? What if I'd let you come pick me up? What if I'd asked someone to walk me to the bus stop? What if? Why me? But it's all useless, pointless, endless torture. It happened, and no amount of wishing or what-ifs will ever change that."

"Jamie—" He was fucking breaking inside and the ragged pieces fell from his eyes in droves. Every one of them burned like hell spilling down his cheeks.

Scooting closer, Jamie brought her tiny hands up and placed them on his face, forcing him to look at her. *Really* look at her. He swore she reached inside and cured the gut rot that had plagued him for the last decade.

"I know you'll understand when I tell you that in order for me to survive this, I need to erase everything about who I used to be. I'm not Jamie Hallow anymore. That girl is dead and gone. But this one right here? She's living. She wants to live. But there's only one way she can, Mike." Her voice was quiet and gentle, holding threads of steely resolve.

She was letting him go.

The irony was they both pined for each other every day they were apart. Now they both needed to cut the same string. It was harder than he thought it would be. Not because he wanted her back. Because he didn't want her to forget him, yet that's exactly what she needed to do.

"So this is good-bye then?" he choked out.

"It has to be," she murmured.

"Please tell me you'll be okay. I can't leave until I know that."

"They broke a lot of things, but not my will to live. Otherwise, I would have never made it out alive. I *will* be okay, Mike. I'll never be the same, but I will be okay. Someday."

"Can I hug you?" he asked. He didn't want to do anything that made her uncomfortable, but he'd been connected to this woman for more than half his life. Just walking away from her with nothing but a sad good-bye didn't seem right.

She looked nervous when she nodded.

"You sure? Because I don't—"

"Yes. Yes," she breathed.

Mike slowly and carefully wound his arms around her slight waist at the same time she let hers fall around the back of his neck. When she was all the way pressed against him, he intentionally kept his hold loose and brought a palm up to cup her head. She laid her cheek on his shoulder. They just breathed.

He didn't know how long they sat like that. Seconds. Minutes, maybe. They were quiet, both lost in their own thoughts while they remembered before erasing each other.

It was a futile attempt, on his part at least. He'd always remember.

"You may forget about me, Jamie, and that's okay. I want you to. But as long as I live, I'll never forget you." *How could he? She'd brought him to Giselle.* With a lingering kiss to the crown of her head, he let her go, standing when she sat back on her heels.

Then without another word he walked out, realizing you can never really leave your past behind because it's already shaped your future.

CHAPTER 19

Giselle

"Eight in the right corner," Mike announced. She couldn't see his face because his back was to her, but she heard the cock and bull in his tone. She could just envision the smug grin stretched on his impossibly beautiful face. The challenge lighting up his cloudy blues.

"That's an impossible shot, fucker. But it's your money, so hey, I'm happy to take it."

"Yeah, I'm probably overreaching," he batted back. It was a lie. Mike had Manny right where he wanted him. It had been as easy as leading a lamb to the slaughter. She felt the glee pinging off his insides like a pinball machine. She stifled a laugh.

Giselle stood right inside the door of the game room and watched—well, ogled—her Fated's fine, tight ass as he bent at the waist and meticulously lined up his shot. When he reared back, she enjoyed the bunch of his triceps, the strength of his hand gripping the cue. Jesus, that man was sexy. So fucking sexy.

And tonight, he was going to be hers.

Ren's statement the other day battled with her will

and had finally won. *"You've been evading anything that resembles a relationship since I've known you."*

He was so right. She had and she was done bobbing and weaving.

She wanted Mike. She wanted *more*. She wanted it all.

Giselle struggled with this decision all day. While it was the right one, it still weighed on her, even now. She had unfinished business. Business she'd had every intention of still following through with up until the moment she held that sweet baby in her arms.

Then a spotlight of an entirely unknown color shined down, drawing a path she didn't even know was possible.

That innocent little girl needed parents, and Giselle didn't want her to go to just any family. Giselle wanted *her and Mike* to be her family. As impossible as it was, she was finally, *finally* ready to be a mate. And a mammi.

That meant, though, giving up revenge. That didn't just feel like a failure, it was unconscionable. But to track Siobhan meant risking her life. It was a risk she was no longer willing to take—now she had too much to live for. She had others she loved, others who depended on her. That still didn't mean it was easy to accept. It wasn't. It might never be. The thought of Siobhan, or those like him, destroying the innocence of little girls, a girl like the one she wanted to raise and protect, was absolutely gut wrenching.

But it was him or her.

She couldn't have both.

And she chose her. For the first time in her life, she chose herself.

A loud whoop cut through her, focusing her attention back on the males in front of her. She laughed softly when she saw Manny reluctantly handing over a hundred.

"How the fuck did you make that?" he asked with a scowl on his face.

"Oh, did I forget to mention you're looking at the BCAPL three-time National 8-Ball Champion?"

"You played me, asshole." Steam practically rose from Manny's ears. He was always a sore loser, especially at pool, which he considered his "calling."

"I didn't play you. I won fair and square," Mike said nonchalantly, stuffing the bill into his black wallet and shoving it back into his pocket.

Manny stalked around the table until he was right in her Fated's face. Looking down his nose, he spat, "You're a fucking pool shark and you just played me."

She stiffened. If that fucker even breathed wrong in Mike's direction, she was going to rain down the fires of brimstone on him before she broke every finger and ripped his balls clean from his body.

Yes...she had a thing for balls. It was the most vulnerable and treasured part of a male's anatomy. Sans his dick.

Mike's spine snapped, not backing down a fraction. "I think you need to find your nut sack, vampire, and take your loss like a man instead of a little bitch."

Oh shit.

Oh *shit*.

The air in the room thickened until she was sure there would be bloodshed. Then Manny threw his head back and laughed, clasping the side of Mike's head in an unyielding grip. "Yep, you'll do just fine, human."

"I don't believe I asked for or needed your approval, vampire."

Manny's smirk grew. He released Mike and flipped his gaze toward Giselle. He knew she'd been there the whole time. Prick. "You can keep him."

"Fuck off, Manny," she gritted. He chuckled under his breath. She wanted to take a pool cue and shove it so far up his ass he'd never quite talk the same again.

"Well, I'm outta here before I'm taken for another hundi. Catch you later," Manny said coolly. He was smart to keep a wide berth as he breezed past Giselle, but not smart enough not to goad her a little more with a smug wink.

"Fucker," she yelled after him, ignoring his laugh.

When she turned back to Mike and his gaze collided with hers, she immediately felt better. His smile practically melted her on the spot. "Hey, baby."

Why did just that look, that voice, those stupid endearing words make her feel better? Because that's love. "Hey," she replied lightly, her own smile taking root.

It took him just a few long strides before he had her back on the wall, her face between his hands and his mouth to hers. "I missed you," he mumbled, caging her in with his bulk.

She'd missed him, too. She'd been gone nearly all day. A hell of a lot longer than she'd expected or planned, but Kate had to practically pry that baby from her grip. She'd fed her, changed her, rocked her. Fell in love with her.

"How was your day?" he asked. It's as if he knew she was as different as she felt.

"It was good. Really good, actually. Yours?"

Giselle wanted to tell him about her, about number one. About her microscopic fingernails and her toothless smile. How her eyes were the color of jade and sucked you into her very soul, wrapping you a million times around her heart. How she kicked her little, bowed legs as if she was pedaling a bike when Giselle changed her diaper. How she was the most perfect thing ever born.

But his mouth descended again on hers after he mumbled, "Just as," and she was just as lost to him as she was to her. When his lips started a trek along her jaw, her body instantly liquefied. "I want you," was a desire-filled call brushing against the shell of her ear.

"I thought you needed help?" she teased softly. He'd told her this morning that he'd become her sex slave and needed to find a sex addicts anonymous support group.

With his hands slowly climbing her torso, inching closer to her now-aching breasts, his lips made their way to the other side of her neck. "Addicts mean well until they need their next fix," he breathed unevenly. "It's all lies. Don't believe me when I tell you that again."

"Well, who am I to push you toward recovery when you're not ready?"

She was just reaching for the fly of his jeans, his hard cock already straining against it, when a throat clearing to her right froze her in place. Leaning his forehead to hers, Mike cursed under his breath. Shit. She should have flashed them out of there back to his place, but was too caught up in the moment. In him. In possibilities that felt more real every second.

"Sorry to interrupt." Ren's voice rumbled next to her. He sounded genuine. "But I need a few minutes of your time."

"Kinda busy here," she retorted snidely, unable to look at him out of sheer embarrassment at almost being caught with her hand in the cookie jar.

"Giselle. It's important." That gave her pause. The gravity of his tone. The use of her full name. The weight of his words. Every hair stood on end.

"Go," Mike said softly before placing a chaste kiss on her lips. "I'll be here when you get back."

They exchanged a look. Ren and Mike. She wondered what passed between them because it was something. Something big.

Oh God.

Why did it feel like yet another shift was about to happen?

"What's wrong?" Giselle demanded after they'd walked down a few doors into a small conference room.

177

"Nothing's *wrong*."

Her eyes narrowed. "If nothing's wrong, what's so goddamned important that you couldn't wait?" she grated, now irritated she didn't tell him to fuck off when she had the chance.

"Sit down." The detached nod he gave in the direction of a chair burned her. And scared the shit of out her.

Please don't say something that's going to fuck up my life, she silently pleaded with him. *Please.*

"I don't need to sit. Just tell me. Whatever it is, just say it straight up."

Taking a step forward, Ren grabbed both her hands. His large palms engulfed hers and her own began to sweat. Swallowing past a lump slowly choking her, she whispered on a rasp, "What the fuck is going on, Ren?" *You're scaring me.*

His flinty eyes stabbed hers, staring, gauging. Power pulsed from him in dense waves. Testosterone dripped thick, like raw honey. Victory shone in the gloss of his enlarged pupils, making him seem more menacing than usual. She recognized the look of triumph. It was almost as if...if he'd just been in battle. *What the...?*

"Siobhan is dead," he declared matter-of-factly.

Siobhan is dead.

Siobhan is dead?

The air suddenly became reedy and hot. Her knees went weak and she almost bit it before Ren had her shoved in a chair. She vaguely noticed he was on one knee in front of her, talking, yet she couldn't hear any noise coming out.

Siobhan is dead.
Siobhan is dead.
Siobhan is dead.
Dead.

That can't be true. She had to have misheard. "What did you say?"

"You heard me, baby girl. Siobhan is dead."

Dead. Could that really be possible? After all this time?

"But...but how? When? I don't understand? And how did you find out?"

Guilt was a funny thing. No matter how old you got or how experienced you were it was an impossible emotion to hide. Tricky to bury. It flickered ever so fast, and if you weren't paying close enough attention, in that one nanosecond, you'd miss it.

Giselle didn't make mistakes like that.

"Ren...what did you do?" she breathed harshly, not sure if she was relieved or mad as fuck he took something that was supposed to be hers.

His lips pursed when he answered, "I did what I had to. It's done now."

"Tell me," she demanded urgently. "Tell me what you did."

Ren's jaw set as hard as his eyes. "I set that motherfucker on fire and watched his flesh and bones turn to ash after I cut his motherfucking head from his shoulders."

Her entire body sagged against the leather cushion. She should be pissed at him for doing this. She should be happy that Siobhan was dead. Rejoicing. At peace. This was something she'd wanted for over a century, yet now all she felt was...numb.

Giselle let her eyes fall to her lap. She wanted to drill Ren into the ground until he told her everything, but strangely, she wasn't really sure it mattered anymore. Her last reason for avoiding the bonding was now gone, truly dead, and even though she thought she'd let it go earlier, it would have always been the tiniest nit in the back of her head. That one small taunt, a fester of regret.

"You're sure? He's really dead?"

He turned her palm up and dumped a heavy, bloody metal pendant into it. "Pretty fucking sure."

The sight made her stomach churn. She turned the ruined family heirloom over and over, trying not to remember the way it hit the back of her head repeatedly when he…

Bloody hell.

"It's really over then?" she asked, breathing deeply while refusing to let herself get dragged down into hellish memories.

"It really is."

They stared at each other. She knew him well. Better than anyone. He was waiting for her to scream and pitch a hissy fit because he avenged her without her permission. Yesterday, she probably would have. But today? Today she'd had an epiphany, so all she felt was immense gratitude that he loved her enough to free her soul this way.

"Thank you," she strangled out. With a slow, deliberate exhale that final toxic part of her life left for good.

"No thanks necessary." Ren stood gracefully, placing a chaste kiss on her forehead on the way up. "So, you have a good day?" He tried to make the conversation light, his face stoic, yet the minute the question was in the air, she *knew*.

With the force of a gale wind, Ren had shoved her toward her Fated, but the brush of a feather was all it took for her to find her daughter.

Sneaky bastard.

She was itching to talk about that little girl. This needed to be a conversation she had with Mike first, though, not Ren, so she diverted.

"Are you ever going to tell me the whole story? How you found him?"

"Some other day. Right now, I think you have someone in the other room who's been unbelievably patient waiting for his Fated to make some pretty big decisions. Don't you?"

A slow smile crept its way across her face and pretty soon she was beaming. Then she did something she rarely did. She threw her arms around Ren's neck and squeezed, pouring every ounce of love she had for her pseudo brother into that hug. "Thank you," she said on a quiet breath.

"For what, baby girl?" he mumbled in her ear, hugging her back as hard.

For being a friend even when I tried pushing you away.

For believing in me when I didn't.

For being willing to kill for me so I could have my chance at happiness, unencumbered.

For everything.

"For saving me from myself."

His chuckle warmed her deep inside. "Don't let all my effort go to waste."

Not a fiery chance in hell.

Giselle had wasted the entire last year denying what could be, but no more. She was home and she was moving in permanently. But she had one last obstacle left to eliminate before she bonded with her rightful mate.

And it would be the hardest thing she'd ever, ever done.

CHAPTER 20

Mike

"You look different," he told her. She *felt* different to him, too. He couldn't put his finger on it exactly, but he'd sensed it the second their eyes met in the pool room earlier. Something in her had changed.

"Different how?" Giselle took a sip from a bottle of water she'd been nursing. She leaned leisurely against the kitchen counter, one hand tucked under the opposite armpit. She was trying to appear relaxed. He knew better. And him being the asshole he was—or maybe just a man thinking with his small head—he could hardly concentrate on anything else but the swell of her breasts playing peekaboo from her low-cut blouse.

Would he always have this visceral physical reaction to her? Hell, who was he kidding? He was a guy. He'd be two hundred and pop an instant woody if she just breathed in his direction.

"Like that invisible weight has finally been lifted."

She smiled then. *Really* smiled. God, it hit him in the center of his chest every fucking time. He'd do anything to make her do that, twenty-four seven.

"It has," she replied, sounding a little surprised herself.

"Come here." Palm up, she gave it a glance before

setting her bottle on the countertop. She sauntered—in that sexy way only she knew how—over to where he sat at the table. The moment her hand touched his he had her between his splayed legs. He pushed up her shirt and started roaming the flat planes of her stomach with his tongue before she could protest. "Wanna tell me about it?" he coaxed between kisses.

He thought she'd say no. Expected to have her pinned to the wood his elbow currently rested on in about five seconds when she surprised him, answering a soft, "Yes."

"Really?" Looking up over her mountainous breasts, her lips were drawn tight, her face serious. Her eyes scared as fuck.

"Yes," she reiterated again. "I want to tell you about it. I want to"—she paused and dove her hands into his hair, lightly rubbing his scalp—"tell you everything."

The hard-on he'd been sporting suddenly died an awful death. His stomach felt sick. *Shit*. This was it. Everything he thought he wanted to know about her past suddenly went out the fucking window. He couldn't bear the tears and agony each mouthful of her torment would bring him. "You sure, baby? We don't have to do this, you know." *We don't ever have to do this if you don't want*, he wanted to add, but didn't. If she needed to do this, he had to let her.

Bottom lip pinched between her upper teeth, she answered with a small bow of her head.

"Okay then." Heart beating a hundred miles a second, he laced their fingers together, leading her into the living room. Settling them on the couch, he kept tight hold of her as much for him as for her. Maybe more.

"So, ah...where do you want to start?" He was finding it hard to breathe already and she hadn't even said one word.

One slim shoulder lifted up. "I guess the only good

place to start is the beginning, right?" *Oh, Giselle.* She was trying to be so brave, but didn't she see that she didn't need to be? That she could strip herself raw and bare and he'd always, always take care of her? Soothe her? Love her?

"Stop anytime you need, yeah?"

"Okay. As much as you may want to interrupt, can I get out what I need to before you say anything?"

It would be hard, but he'd try. "Sure."

With a fleeting smile, she took a deep breath and began. "My mammi died giving birth to me. And as you know, once your mate dies, you follow shortly thereafter, so within a few days, my pappi passed. My brothers, Cato and Aeneas raised me. Cato was the eldest, thirty-five years my senior. Aeneas was twenty years when I was born. He'd just completed his final blooding only days before.

"My brothers took my parents' deaths hard, as you can imagine. I was living and they were dead because of me. And they never let me forget it. When I was eight, I found a letter my pappi had written me on his deathbed telling me he made them promise to care for me, love me, and give me the life he and Mammi would have."

Her voice cracked ever so slightly, but she continued undaunted.

"But they didn't. They hated me. Told me every day I was lucky they let me take another breath. I was death, a stain on the family name. I often wondered why they didn't just kill me. Why they blooded me at all when they could have just let me die, but as I grew older I heard stories of our pappi. He was an honored, revered male. A pillar of the community. He founded our village, made it a refuge for the lost and the broken. He was truly a great male.

"The more I understood our family's importance in our village, the more I understood killing me would have drawn the kind of attention they didn't want. So on the outside, my brothers pretended we were the perfect little happy family and they were the overprotective older siblings. On the inside, though, it was anything but."

She paused briefly, unable to hide the wistfulness in her tone. Then with a big sigh, she started again.

"My life was the very definition of hell on Earth. I wished I'd been the one who had died instead of my parents. I begged them often to just kill me and get it over with. But my death would have ruined their standing, their reputations, risked Cato's seat on the council, which he took over from my pappi. They were rarely physically abusive—it was emotional and verbal, but they'd saved the worst of themselves for when I was older. Because they had better plans for me. It all became very apparent shortly after my fifteenth birthday."

Looking him straight in the eye, she added, "After a female vampire's second blooding, her biological changes are swift and...very noticeable."

Oh fuck, no. *Nooo.* He wanted to stop her. Stop this. He knew exactly where this vile story was headed. He felt his blood burn black and his thoughts turn murderous. The thunderous roar in his ears was so deafening he barely heard her next mumbled sentence.

"...they began to 'farm me out,' if you will, so I could earn my keep."

Jesus. Fucking. Christ.

No. No. No.

She kept going. He struggled to listen when all he wanted to do was shut out the toxic confession.

Every evenly spoken syllable was bludgeoning torture.

Every brave sentence strung together another layer of skin flayed.

Every stoic page an unbelievable tale of horror that made his ears bleed and his gut twist.

Mike's stomach cramped like he had food poisoning, only it was word poisoning instead.

He dug deep for grit he didn't know he had while she purged for what felt like hours. She kept her head high and her eyes dry. How? He had no fucking idea. But he'd been right. She *was* the strongest person he knew. She was titanium. Any lesser creature would have been crushed under the oppressive weight of what she bore, young and all alone.

The only saving grace was that every last one of those motherfuckers was dead. Including the one who got away. The one Ren had told him about. Because if they weren't? He'd find them. He'd cut their hands off so they were helpless. He'd gouge their eyes out so they couldn't see. He'd destroy them until they begged for mercy. Except he'd give none. He'd make them suffer in perpetuity. He'd make them wish for death, knowing their souls rotting in hell would be a better fate than the wrath of Mike Thatcher.

Now things made so much more sense.

Her hesitation. Her excuses. Her defensive and cold façade. Keeping everyone at arm's length, because if your family betrayed and used and defiled you, who the fuck could you trust?

At some point he'd tugged her onto his lap, not giving her a choice in the matter. With her ensconced safely in his arms, he tenderly stroked her hair...held her a little too tight. He could hardly stop breathing in her scent or take his lips from her temple. He connected them every single place humanly possible.

She was real.

She was here.

She was a survivor.

She talked until her throat was hoarse, but Giselle never broke.

He did, though. He had no shame that he cried quiet tears of anguish, which soaked into her hair. She had to have felt them but she didn't call him out. Instead, she snuggled closer, needing their linking as badly he did.

When she'd been quiet for a few minutes, there was one question she hadn't answered and he *had* to ask. He didn't want to, but it would kill him not to know. His vocal cords felt strangled, the heinous name barely able to be pushed out. "Xavier?"

She hummed a noise in the back of her throat that made bile rise. He should have kept his mouth shut. "Never mind," he choked.

"No, it's okay." She tilted her head and locked her gaze on his for the first time since she began. Bringing a hand up, she placed it gently on his face, stroking her thumb over the apple of his cheek. He realized she was wiping away his tears.

Jesus, his heart exploded with love. His eyes and nose pricked with a fresh wave of sadness. She was the one who went through unspeakable horrors, yet here *she* was trying to comfort *him*.

Unbelievable.

She spoke then, her voice soft, her gaze now focused far away. Stuck somewhere in the past again. "No one touched me physically. Well, not in *that* way at least. They did beat me pretty badly, but it was all a big mind-fuck mostly. There was a vampire with some skill I'd never heard of. He possessed part of my skill, mind sifting, but it was so far advanced. And mine doesn't work on other vampires. His did. He could dig into your darkest thoughts, excavate your most painful memories, and make you relive every agonizing second of them. Of course, you can imagine what he found. It felt so real and I..."

Fuck. No wonder she stayed away from him for so long after that.

"Stop." He didn't need her to finish. While his entire body sagged in intense relief that no one had violated her again, he was done. Felt like the dried-up pulp left behind from a squeezed orange. "Don't say anything else," he whispered on a broken breath. "Please. I'm not sure I can take any more right now." Or ever.

Mike was lost for words or thoughts. He was incredibly sad for but immensely proud of Giselle. The woman he was meant to live and die for could have just as easily chosen to give up rather than fight. That she didn't was a testament to the kind of spirit that lived inside her, even back then. She was a warrior through and through, and he almost felt as though he didn't deserve her.

Wrapped around each other, they sat silent. He lost track of time, choosing to revel in the simple things: Her warm exhales hitting his chest. The silk of her hair between his fingers. The faint scent of vanilla and...*baby powder?*...on her skin.

Then a sick feeling twisted his innards until they were tied in a thousand knots. "I'm sorry," he said.

"Don't say that. I don't want your pity. That's why I didn't want to talk about—"

"No, that's not what I'm sorry for, although I won't tell you I'm not sorry all that shit happened to you, Giselle, because...fuck. I am. So goddamned sorry." With a finger hooked under her chin, he lifted her eyes to his. "But now I am sorry about how hard I pushed you in the bedroom. I should have asked. I—"

She set a finger to his moving lips. "Don't be sorry. I needed it. And you haven't done anything I don't like. You, ah..." When her gaze darted away, embarrassment colored her cheeks. It was damn endearing because Giselle did not do embarrassment.

Kissing that finger still resting on his mouth, he prodded gently, "I what, baby?"

"YouwerethefirstmaleIvebeenwithsinceIgotfree," she mumbled, squirming a little on his lap.

Huh?

"What?"

"You heard me."

"Uh, baby, you sounded like Charlie Brown's parents. I couldn't make out a stitch of that garbled mess."

She huffed in annoyance. He wanted to laugh, but he really wanted to know what turned her beautiful face a nice hue of pink even more.

"I said, you were the first male I've been with since I got free."

Her sentence still ran together and he mentally worked to unwrap her puzzled message. When he thought he had, he needed to confirm it since he still couldn't have heard her right. "What did you just say?"

"Stop it." She swatted his chest playfully. "You heard me, asshole."

"You really haven't been with anyone since you slaughtered those motherfuckers?" he asked incredulously.

Her eyes shifted again and he gently grabbed her chin, directing her back to him. He patiently waited for her to respond.

"That would be correct," she admitted in a small voice.

Holy shit. *Giselle hadn't had a sexual partner for over a hundred twenty years?* No wonder she'd felt like a virgin. She was one in every way that mattered. A swell of primal male possessiveness welled, his cells soaking it in like a dry sponge until he felt like banging his chest with meaty fists in the treetops yelling victory. Against his will, his cock involuntarily started joining the party, too. *Down boy. Down.* Now *is not the time.*

Back to her.

"Then how did you feed?" He knew for vampires, sex and blood went together like peanut butter and jelly or Sonny and Cher, so how the hell did she feed if she hadn't had sex in over one hundred fucking years?

The color on her face deepened. "Bagged blood mostly."

His brows rose in question. "Mostly?"

"Sometimes I'll feed from one of the females at Dev's club." She acted like it wasn't a big deal, but again...PB&J.

"Female? Did you, uh..." Oh hell, yes. *Please* say yes.

"Jesus, you perv." She laughed. "No, I haven't had sex with anyone—male *or* female."

"Well now that's a damn shame," he drawled. "You could have just let my imagination run wild, you know."

"You're such a male." Her words scolded him, yet her tone was light and playful.

"Yeah, and I don't hear you complaining."

Swooping down, he captured her lips between his, kissing her sweetly and with the utter reverence she deserved. Giselle moaned, shifting on his lap until she straddled him. He held her face and deepened the connection but didn't plan to take tonight any further. He felt as though he were swimming in an emotional cesspool, his strokes sluggish but measured so he didn't drown. Tonight was about tenderness. He needed like hell to hold her and remind himself that she was, in fact, real, she was his, and he was the luckiest son-of-a-bitch on planet Earth to have a beauty like her wind him up like a top.

Only Giselle had other ideas.

And fuck if he could refuse her. He'd never refuse her a damn thing.

"I want you to be mine," she whispered against his jaw before unleashing her fangs, scraping them erotically down his throat. Twin lines of blood welled, dripping, and he grew impossibly, painfully hard when she ran her tongue back up, lapping every stray drop.

"Jesus Christ, Giselle." That move right there had the ability to make him lose his man card, his seed already coaxed halfway up his shaft. Palming her head, he stopped her short before he had to hand it over. "We can wait. I don't want to pressure you."

"I don't want to wait anymore. I want to start living."

"You sure?" His question was more of a groan as she reached between them and starting undoing the mechanics on his jeans. In a flash, she had his cock out and in her soft hand and was trying her damnedest to revoke his manhood. *Draw on your reserve, Thatcher. Think of Halo, firing your weapon, the zombiepocalypse, for God's sake. Any fucking thing besides the fact you want to coat her hand with your seed.*

"Giselle, stop." With his hand on top of hers, he squeezed hard, forcing her still.

"You don't want—"

"Oh yeah, I want. But I'm going to be buried to the fucking hilt in that sweet pussy when I make you mine. I'm not coming in your hand and if you don't stop, that's exactly what will happen."

"Oh," she breathed heavily, her chest heaving up and down.

"Bed. Now."

Picking her up, she buried her head in his neck and snaked her long, lean legs around his waist. Seconds later, his dick throbbing hard, he lowered her onto his bed. *Their* bed.

"Get naked," he commanded thickly, taking quick care of himself.

He wanted to consume her. Devour and own. But with their clothes thrown haphazardly all over the bedroom, Mike took a moment to let his gaze trail over the ethereal goddess currently spread out on his ivory sheets.

Flames of desire licked her cerulean blues, turning them smoky. She palmed her breasts, restlessly pressed her legs together trying to relieve her ache. Her body writhed in a tantalizing mixture of seduction and enchantment. If he wasn't so fucking insane to be inside of her, he could just sit and watch her like this for hours upon hours and never tire.

He wanted to treat her like blown glass and fuck her hard into next year all in the same breath. But he had a feeling this wouldn't be a tender, sweet-gesture-filled lovemaking session. This was going to be a swift, violent, you-belong-to-me-and-only-me, primal coupling.

And the second Giselle spread her legs and begged him to claim her, his patience shattered, the rabid animal inside breaking violently from its leash.

She. Was. His.

He pounced.

He plunged.

He pillaged.

He owned her mouth and her body with equal passion and intent. He sipped her cries and ingested her moans. They tasted like sweetly spun sugar on his taste buds and he let them linger before he swallowed. He climbed inside her, caged her heart, and seized her soul.

He took and took and took until she gave him everything she had. And the second her walls started clenching around his dick, he took that, too. He claimed every flutter and pulse and drop of her climax. He then claimed the next and the next and the one after that until they were all his. Until she was mindless, the only thought being the next release she could catch.

Mike's tempo slowed while he let her catch her breath. But she didn't need it. Her mouth was at his neck, right over his carotid, sucking. While his one thumb was busy playing her taut nipple, the other hand slipped under her neck. He held her there against him, sure and steady. His cock swelled in impatience and every drag in and out of her tight channel lured him closer to the ledge he wanted to free fall from. "Now," he pleaded. Fuck. *Now*.

There was no superfluous preamble. No sweet words, no declarations of love or forevers. She struck like lightning, plunging those razor-sharp teeth into his vein, setting off the most explosive orgasm he'd had to date.

On a pleasure-pained roar, he came. Hard and fast and long. It was devastating. He had no idea what the fuck she'd done, but it went on and on, the ecstasy washing through him in strong pulls until he almost blacked out.

Then her wrist was at his mouth; the tangy flavor of copper coated his tongue. Release after release, or maybe it was just one long, endless—fucking endless—climax kept his blood on fire and his head wrapped in fuzz.

Mine, mine, mine was the never-ending cacophony of their collective voices twisting inside his brain until it spiraled downward and settled in the pit of his black soul.

As Giselle's lifeblood coursed through his bloodstream, any imperfection that resided inside him knit together along the way. He swore to God he felt his cells split and regenerate. He was sure his skin tightened, his senses honed. His muscles thickened, his jaw ached, his bones lengthened. His mind was sharper than a tack.

It was power.

He was power.

He was King, Sultan, Czar.

He was a swirling mass of a hundred thousand volts of unalloyed electrons and if the Prince of Darkness himself stood before him, there was no shred of doubt Mike would win a duel to the death.

Stop, Giselle's voice whispered in his head. *Stop*.

Mike knew exactly what she was demanding. Even through the hazy fog of omnipotence, he yielded to her even though he didn't want to. She was now his nucleus. He revolved around her.

The second his mouth left her wrist he plummeted. The fall was just as swift as the rise. The sharp edge of his orgasm immediately dulled, then waned altogether. His muscles felt atrophied and, unable to hold himself up, he slumped on top of her.

His eyes fell shut. He felt his body roll. He had to take care of her, of his queen, but he was so damn tired he couldn't move. Couldn't think. Could barely breathe.

"Sleep", her sultry voice coaxed.

"I need to take care of you." Did he speak out loud?

"No arguments. You need sleep."

Just for a minute, he thought to himself. *Maybe* just for a minute.

This time, when sleep wound her tempting fingers around him and pulled tight, he fell into her knowing that when he woke he would be a brand new man.

A better man.

The one he was always meant to be.

A vampire's mate.

CHAPTER 21

4 weeks later...

Giselle

"Breathe." She shivered as her mate's lips brushed against the shell of her ear. His hands rested lightly on her hips and she couldn't help but press herself back into him. Mike seemed to have his wits about him. She hoped they rubbed off on her. She could use a whole boatload of them about now. "No need to be nervous, baby."

"Like you're any better," she chided in a hushed voice. She felt the tension coiled inside him.

"We're going to be fine," he said quietly, thoroughly meaning it. He was so sure, so confident, but how could he be? This would be like the blind leading the blind. Neither of them had a clue what they were doing. There really should be a licensing process for this, she'd decided. Mandatory training classes, annual recertification, board exams. How was it possible to suddenly inherit responsibility for another life without a sole qualification? No wonder there were so many fucked-up people roaming around.

"Besides, we have a village of help," he added with conviction.

There was that. Weeks ago when Giselle originally had this crazy-ass idea, she was bound and determined to do it on her own. Well, her and her mate. She didn't want help from others because help equated to failure and failure led to judgment. But she'd come to realize the kind of assistance and advice given to her by Kate, Sarah, and Analise was out of some weird affection and understanding, not scrutiny or derision.

Giselle and Mike stood beside her crib, watching her sleep, watching her breath. Making sure they were there the second she woke up and needed them. Mainly they just stood there in awe of her.

Jade.

Their daughter.

The morning after bonding, Giselle talked to Mike about baby number one. She'd been nervous, not knowing how he'd feel about it, particularly after they'd just become mates. They had so much to learn about each other and throwing a new baby in the mix might not be the best of ideas, but no matter what she did, she couldn't let the idea go without at least talking to him about it.

She should have known better, though. Mike was supportive. Encouraging even.

"Something's on your mind. What is it?"

"Reading my thoughts already?" she hummed *against his neck. She ran her hands down his strong back, scraping her nails against his flesh on the way back up. She'd never get used to how heavenly his nakedness felt against hers or how perfectly his body weight pinned her beneath him.*

"No, but I've been reading your emotions for weeks and I know you're anxious about something. What is it?"

She pulled back, surprised. "You've been feeling my emotions?"

His lips quirked. God, that smug look hooked her every time. "Yep."

"Why didn't you tell me?"

"Because I didn't really understand what it was at first and besides, even if I did, you weren't ready to hear it."

She diverted her eyes, but he gently grabbed her chin and brought her back. "Spill," he quietly encouraged.

Well...here goes nothing. "I met someone." His eyes bugged and she laughed, realizing how that sounded. "She's tiny and sweet and vulnerable and all alone. She's..." Giselle paused, trying to find the right words. "...absolute perfection."

"Yes," he mumbled sweetly against her mouth before taking it in a searing kiss.

"I haven't even asked you anything yet."

"You don't need to, baby. If she brings out this blinding blaze inside you, that's all that matters."

The genuine excitement she'd felt when she'd talked about Jade was infectious. They'd decided together, though, that it would be best to wait just a while. Mike needed time to adjust to his rapidly changing body. She estimated he'd gained about fifty pounds of pure muscle over the course of the last few weeks and if she'd thought he was insanely sexy before, he was a demigod now. Vampire looked awfully fucking good on him. She was damp just thinking about how taut and virile he was. Everywhere.

"You'd better stop thinking those salacious thoughts,

my mate, or I'll have to have to take you in the other room and fuck them out of you."

"You make that sound like a bad thing," she taunted silently.

"I feel like you're challenging my manhood, baby."

"And if I am?"

They'd no sooner taken half a step in the direction of their bedroom when Jade stirred, making those cute little sleep noises that she did when she dreamed. They froze, all thoughts of lust and toe-curling sex evaporating in a flash.

"Cockblocked by my own daughter. Ouch. I suppose I'd better get used to that, huh?" His chuckle slid all the way to her now wet and ready core.

"I think we just need to learn to take advantage of when she naps, instead of staring at her."

"Or we can just get a babysitter."

"To have sex?" she asked incredulously.

"It's called *date night*, baby."

"We just brought her home yesterday. I don't think we need a date night already."

"And I haven't been inside you yet today. That's unacceptable, mate."

She turned in his arms and wound her limbs around his neck. The love she saw floored her. She was pretty sure it always would. "I love you, Mike. Thank you for this. For her."

Pushing some stray hairs behind her ear, he said, "I wanted her as much as you did, Giselle."

While they'd decided they needed to wait to make things official, they'd spent all of their free time with Jade over the past few weeks. They'd bonded as a family well before they officially were and when it became harder and harder to leave her behind at night, they knew it was time.

So yesterday they finally brought their sweet baby girl home.

And insecurities reared their ugly, vicious heads once again.

"What if I'm too lenient?"

"Then I'll be the disciplinarian," he answered plainly.

"What if I'm too strict?"

"Then I'll be the favorite," he chuckled in jest. That made her smile. He probably would be anyway.

"What if she gets you wrapped around her pinky finger?"

"She already has, just like her mammi," he breathed.

Oh God. She's a mammi.

Her stomach flipped in excitement, but nerves piggybacked on top, making her feel sick.

"What if I can't love her like she deserves?" she barely whispered. She was barely getting the hang of being a mate, let alone a parent. It was a daunting, overwhelming, disheartening thought.

He cupped a cheek and bore his gaze into hers. She knew this look. Steely determination. She loved this side of him the most. If not for his grit, they wouldn't be bonded. If not for his insistent, gentle prodding, she would have talked herself out of adopting this perfect little being.

"Not. Fucking. Possible. If your love for her is a tenth of what it is for me, she'll be the luckiest girl in the whole world." It was. It *is*.

A smile tried to break free. He always knew the right thing to say to squash the negative into mush. "You can't swear around her, you know. I read that kids are like sponges. They absorb everything. We don't want her first word to be fuck."

Mike's lips curled in amusement. "Hmmm. Maybe you'll have to punish me until I get it right."

"That sounds like a good reinforcement technique," she hummed.

His eyes fell to her bottom lip, watching his thumb rub it back and forth, back and forth. His attention had shifted solely to her, but hers was still on Jade. "What if I mess up?"

Hot lips met her mouth. "We both will," he mumbled, washing out her moan. "And then we'll make it right again."

The next insecurity was almost out when the softness of sheets surrounded her and her clothes were being ripped off. "Mike..."

He came flush with her, pinning her arms above her head. Her sex went liquid, her nipples strained, needing his mouth, and her body started moving for him. She'd let him dominate her before, but now that his strength almost equaled hers, there was no *letting* about it. He dominated every single part of her, pushing her to her limits but never over. "Every protest is another second without me inside that sweet, wet, tight body, Giselle," he replied on a heave. "Is that what you want?"

She shook her head. *No, no, that isn't what I want.*

"Good." Reaching down, he freed his velvety steel rod and without even removing his jeans, slid inside in one long drive, the denim abrading her bare thighs. When he hit the end of her womb he groaned but stilled. "Besides, we only have half an hour before we need to wake her anyway. The guest of honor can't be late to her own party."

The *baby shower.*

Christ, how could she have forgotten?

"And don't look like that. You know you're excited about it."

"I am not," she protested.

"Yeah, you are," he breathed into her neck as he began moving in the most delicious of ways. He had her panting in short order, her objections now halfhearted at best. "I overheard you talking to Jade about it."

"I was...just...warning her." Giselle gasped her reply between pumps that were getting rougher and quicker with each shift of his hips. She was already balancing precariously on the tip of a climax that was beginning to wash through her.

Her eyes fluttered open when he stilled again. She was overflowing with protests now that had nothing to do with balloons, presents, oohs and ahhs, and unwanted attention.

"Remember what I said about lying?"

Shit. The rat bastard.

"Yeah, that's what I thought." No, he wasn't a rat bastard. He was a smug bastard. "I know how much you enjoy your orgasms, baby."

It didn't take her mate long to find and withhold the one thing that would get her to confess anything and everything, every fucking time.

Moving again, he was slow. Too slow. Too teasing. Too effortless to give her that final push. His curved, wicked mouth hovered over one erect bud, waiting. She knew exactly what he had in mind. It was his favorite spot to feed from her. And for some ungodly reason, his mouth suckling at her breast threw her into a wild orgasm like nothing else.

"Okay, fine. I may be the teeniest tiniest bit excited," she confessed. Deliriously, stupidly, unreasonably excited. No one had ever thrown a party for her before, and even if it was for Jade it was also for her, too. "Happy?"

"Oh yeah. I'm deliriously"—nip—"stupidly"—nip—"unreasonably"—nip— "happy."

"God, you're such an asshole," she chided, but there was no truth behind it. She loved that she didn't have to keep anything from him. That she could be who she was and when she strayed, when she felt unworthy and scared, he'd find her and bring her back to him, reminding her she was loved now and forever.

"I know, but I'm your asshole, right?"

Yes was but a perishable thought because his teeth had now pierced her flesh and she was coming apart at the seams, trying hard not to scream Mike's name, waking their daughter prematurely.

Next time she'd need to try harder. Jade's angry wail filled the house and Mike's frustrated panting filled her ears. "You've got to be kidding me," he mumbled against her tightened nipple, flicking it hard with his tongue.

"I'm sorry," she moaned, still mostly lost in her postorgasmic haze. "I'll get her."

One last pull then he licked the tiny punctures closed and bounded off the bed, leaving her cold and empty, but satisfied and smiling.

"I'll get her."

She loved her baby girl more than her next heartbeat, but not having her mate all to herself anytime she wanted would definitely take some getting used to. She may have to rethink this "date night" idea. "You sure?" she asked, stretching her arms above her head teasingly, letting the hair she'd pulled through her fingers fan out around her.

An arm came down on either side of her head. His mouth swooped in to take hers. Her blood hummed and her body immediately came alive. "I'm sure, you wicked temptress. Now, take a quick shower and get ready to be fawned over." Her mouth turned down at that sickening thought. "And maybe practice turning that frown upside-down." He laughed as he strode nude out of their room.

"Hey, you can't let her see your junk flopping around. You'll scar her!" she yelled after him. His only reply was to laugh harder, but it still didn't drown out Jade's short, high, escalating cries.

Giselle stayed still, waiting with anxiousness until their little girl's cries abruptly stopped. Then she heard Mike's low, gruff voice soothing her. Telling her she'd cost him an orgasm and that his balls were bluer than the Pacific. Then she heard him tell her he was going to gag her mammi next time they had sex so they could finish without Giselle's wails waking her up.

Oh my God.

What the hell kind of parents were they going to be if they walked around naked and talked about sex in front of their daughter?

"Fucking good ones," her mate's growly voice echoed in her head. *"Now...get that fine ass in the shower and stop stalling."*

"But..."

"No buts, baby. Everyone's waiting."

"Fine," she grumbled, knowing there was no way out of this absurd human ritual.

Epilogue

Everyone was there. The whole fucking gang and then some. All the Lords and their mates, of course. Ren, Thane, Manny. All the lieutenants. Hell, even Geoffrey and Rom's brother, Taiven, were here, huddled in the corner discussing something that seemed serious. And if she wasn't mistaken, there were a few females from the shelter who she may have grunted at once or twice in passing because she had no choice.

This entire thing was out of control.

It was supposed to be a "small" event, according to Sarah. "Just a few people," Sarah said. Since when did a few mean thirty? "Just an hour," she'd told Giselle. They were now going on two. "Just light finger food and a couple of gifts for Jade." Shit, there was enough food here to feed a small village for a week and presents upon presents littered the entire length of two eight-foot tables, spilling onto the floor all around them. Did babies need all that crap?

Asinine.

She was shaking her head at what she let herself be talked into when Ren moseyed up beside her. "You look like you're ready to breathe fire," he mused on a laugh.

"I think they're doing this on purpose," she spat back. She'd taken up residence across the room lest she rip someone's hair out. Three "someone's" hairs, to be exact. Don't think she hadn't thought of it, had it not come with the repercussion of punishment by their mates.

"Doing what?" He knew exactly "what."

"This," she whisper-yelled, gesturing wildly around the room where it looked like a party threw up. Muted sheer fabric hung in arches from the ceiling. There were stupid welcome banners, baby blocks, stuffed animals, pink and purple balloons, streamers, and cupcakes that had princess cutouts on top. Fucking princesses. Her daughter was going to learn to wield a sword like a soldier and employ sarcasm as a first language. She was *not* going to be sitting around singing Disney songs, playing with dolls, and emulating The Little fucking Mermaid for Christ's sake.

Did humans really do this to their kids and each other? It was overkill. Appalling, actually.

"I think it's cute."

"Cute? There's so much goddamned pastel in here I think I fell into an Easter egg."

"They mean well, Elle." His voice held an air of amusement, which pissed her off more.

"You're enjoying the fuck out of this, aren't you?"

He chuckled without apology. "Just a bit."

Mike caught her eye and winked knowingly but didn't make a move toward her. He was hovering over their daughter instead, knowing she wouldn't want both of them too far away yet also understanding why Giselle had disengaged from this ridiculous melee. It was ultimately for her own safety.

"She's stunning, your daughter."

Her tension eased a bit and she allowed a small grin on her lips. "I know."

"You're going to be a great mammi, Elle," he told her quietly.

Breaking her gaze from how sweetly and longingly Analise held her daughter, she looked at her longtime friend—the male responsible for her little slice of happiness. "You think?"

He nodded just once.

A deep breath later, she replied softly, "Thanks for saying that." She needed the confidence boost.

"Not saying anything that's untrue."

No one, except maybe Ren, would have thought this was possible, including her. Yet here she was.

A bonded mate.

A terrified, but elated mammi.

Even fighting the pull to become some semblance of a *friend* with the other females in her life. She had to give in, she told herself. It's clear they weren't going anywhere. Her entire world had been upended but in the best possible way.

A sudden flurry by the "queens" grabbed her attention. She watched them hand the baby back to Mike and begin to gather pens and papers and a basket filled with all sorts of baby stuff in it while they chattered away, trying to herd the crowd into chairs. Throwing worried glimpses her way.

Giselle's skin started prickling. The tight threesome had apparently made Sarah their sacrificial lamb, knowing she was the least likely of the bunch to get her head bitten off, so when Sarah first mentioned a baby shower in passing to Giselle, her immediate response had been no. Well, "when pigs fucking fly," was more accurate. But when she talked to Mike about it, he swayed her decision.

"It's for Jade, not you."

"Oh."

"Let them do it, baby. You're gonna have to do a lot of things you don't want to when you have kids. Might as well start off parenthood with a bang."

So after she'd educated herself on what a baby shower entailed, she'd acquiesced. But she'd been adamant she didn't want them going to any trouble and she unequivocally did not want fluff. They hadn't listened because the entire damn party felt like she'd been dropped into a rainbow forest of gumdrop trees and cotton candy. But she could handle all of this, as nauseating as it was. The one thing she would go ballistic over was the one she'd been especially clear on.

No *games.*

No. Fucking. Games.

So the fact that Sarah was now grinning wide and mischievous did not bode well. For Sarah. Or the other two.

"Uh oh," Ren whispered. He stiffened and took a big step to his right. Away from her.

"I swear to God if they ask me to—"

"Giselle, it's time for games!" Sarah quipped, her eyes alight with devilry.

Oh, hell to the thirteenth no. That little witch. "Heads are going to roll. I'm going to murder the mate of a Lord," she muttered low and even. "You realize you're going to have to raise Jade, now, right?"

Ren burst out laughing, doubling over, and Mike's gaze latched onto hers seconds before she blew. One side of his mouth was twisted and his bushy brows were halfway up his forehead.

"Jade," he mouthed. "Do it for your daughter."

Fucking hell.

Will he always pull that card?

"Yes," his voice whispered in her ear. *"Need to practice a bit on that frown upside-down, baby."* He chuckled, but this time, it was out loud. Asshole was getting a huge kick out of this.

Jade. Jade. Do it for Jade, she kept repeating, although she didn't see what a pointless game had to do with Jade. Giselle was sure it was just to spite her because they knew they could get away with it and she couldn't retaliate. Directly, anyway.

Blowing out a frustrated breath and containing a

massive eye roll, she pushed off the wall she'd been leaning against and headed across the room, stopping in front of her mate. Mike placed Jade in her arms. The instant that beauty's bottomless green pools landed on hers, she melted into goo and forgot everything else.

She smiled and cooed and humbly kowtowed herself to the precious bundle she held close. She was a different female around her daughter: calm, relaxed.

Well...mostly.

Settling in the corner of the couch, Mike at her side, she pulled herself away from the baby in her arms and pinned her traitorous "friend" with a hateful glare. Friend, her ass. Friends didn't backstab each other, did they? Cuz it felt like the knife of duplicity was wedged pretty damn deep between her ribs right now.

"I thought I explicitly said no games," she said tartly to Sarah.

"Did you say that? I don't remember having that conversation," she replied smoothly. Bitch's eyebrows even bent inward to round out her faked confusion. The sharp tang of her lie hung in the air between them and the entire room fell silent. Everyone was holding a breath to see what Giselle was going to do next. But when Rom came to Sarah's side and slung a protective arm around her shoulder, saying jovially, "Probably not a good idea to egg her on, beauty," Giselle decided the quickest and easiest route out of here was to just play along.

"Let's get this shit over with," she grumbled, bouncing a now tired, fussy girl on her shoulder.

"That's the spirit," Sarah replied with a cheeky wink. Kate and Analise breathed a visible sigh of relief, jumping up to begin distributing pens and paper to everyone.

Mike leaned over and the promise he whispered roughly in her ear sent skitters of desire down her spine. "You're doing real good, baby. Just a bit longer and we can make our escape. Then I'm going to pick up right where we left off before we were interrupted."

"Yeah?" A fire was already starting to rage between the middle of her thighs at the very thought.

"Oh yeah. But you'll need to be quiet this time so we can finish properly."

"And if I can't?" She taunted him with a grin. Thinking about him gagging her had messed with her head. That's practically all she'd been thinking about since the second he said it to their daughter.

"I have ways," he whispered.

"I like ways," she encouraged, knowing he was reading her thoughts.

He kissed her sweetly on the lips. Before she might have, but now she didn't even care about the PDA. She liked that he felt comfortable projecting his love for her in public. "You look happy," he said, his smile lazy.

She glanced around the room, gaze landing on each and every person. Like a hawk, Dev tracked every move his pregnant mate made. Sarah was perched on Rom's lap. The unmated males grumbled, drinking their beers and eyeing the exit longingly. She could relate. The other females sat together on the loveseat, watching everyone with interest.

They'd all gathered here for her and her mate. It didn't matter everyone was trying to convince her this was for Jade. Jade would never remember this. It was for *her*. Becoming a mammi was a big deal. It was a moment to celebrate, especially for someone who never had a chance at being one.

"What the fuck, kitten?" Damian protested loudly. "I thought you said we were just going to have a few snacks and watch the Sox play?"

Turns out she wasn't the only one duped.

"Is that what she told you to get you here?" Rom said, his voice nearly a bark. "I think maybe your mate needs a reprimand."

"Oh, she'll get one, all right," he replied low and dark and promising. Analise just threw an impudent grin his way and moved on, narrowly avoiding the fingers trying to snag her. She had to hand it to Analise. Not one other female she'd ever met could tame the egotistical Damian DiStephano, yet Analise had him square under four-inch stilettos and Damian never once complained. His adoration for her bled through every action. Months ago it made her sick. Now she got it.

Damian caught her watching, offering a small smile. An olive branch, of sorts. It was a big gesture for him. One he'd not have proposed before meeting his mate. Guess mates can change even the toughest of vamps. She would know.

Giselle decided to return it, wanting to put their sordid past to bed once and for all.

These were her people. This was her life, her future. And even though she may not always deserve it, everyone in this room, even Damian, would have her back if needed. They would care for her child as their own if she and her mate couldn't. For better or worse, this was her family. And for the first time in her life, she was starting to understand the true value of what that meant.

It was something she'd never had. But her daughter would have it. Jade would be raised with adoration and acceptance and respect. She'd have a real home filled with genuine family and unconditional love.

Turning her attention back to Mike, she initiated the press of their lips, this time just as Sarah started yipping about the rules of the game she was forcing down their throats. Even though it irritated the shit out of her and she just wanted to be alone with her new family, she had to reluctantly admit she wouldn't change a thing about this moment.

Smiling against her mate's mouth, there was no possible answer she could give but, "I've never been happier in my life."

EVADING

Giselle wasn't one for prophetic thoughts but she knew deep in her being that sometimes you have to drown in the darkness before you can bathe in the light. Although she'd been drowning for over a hundred years, she'd gladly do it a hundred more if they were the prizes that waited at the end of her suffering.

Mike and Jade were more than worth it.

~ THE END ~

My musical inspiration for writing
Evading:

"I Am The Fire" by Halestorm
"Living Dead Girl" by Rob Zombie
"The Vengeful One" by Disturbed
"Broken Pieces" by Apocalyptica
"Mrs. Hyde" by Halestorm
"Sex Metal Barbie" by In This Moment
"Mayhem" by Halestorm
"Sick Like Me" by In This Moment
"Hate Love" by Adelitas Way
"Love Bites" by Halestorm
"So Cold" by Breaking Benjamin
"Apocalyptic" by Halestorm
"The Red" by Chevelle
"The Light" by Disturbed
"Warrior" by Evans Blue
"Impossible" by Lacy Sturm
"Fire It Up" by Thousand Foot Crutch
"In Chains" by Shaman's Harvest
"Hush" by Hellyeah

Other Works by K. L. Kreig

PARANORMAL ROMANCE/EROTIC

The **Regent Vampire Lords** series:

Surrendering
Belonging
Reawakening
Evading

CONTEMPORARY ROMANCE/EROTIC

The Colloway Brothers series:

Forsaking Gray
Undeniably Asher
Luke's Absolution
Destination Connelly (releasing summer 2016)

Babbles...

First of all, a huge thank you to the readers who love my Lords and wanted more of Mike and Giselle's story. They were never intended to have their own book, but you all fell in love with them as much as I did. Thank you for your infinite patience while I worked to rid myself of other characters so I could give theirs the focus they deserved.

When I first started writing *Surrendering*, I honestly never meant for Mike to be a reoccurring character in *Belonging*, but I fell hopelessly in love with him. And it wasn't until *Belonging* that I started seeing the "possibilities" between him and Giselle, so I quickly went back and rewrote parts of *Surrendering* to subtly build that tenuous connection between the two.

Giselle always had a harrowing story. It was hard to tell. It was hard to write. It was hard to feel her emotions. I actually shed a lot of tears writing some of her memories and deep feelings of inadequacy so many of us feel because of circumstances beyond our control. She's crusty, she's damaged and life's circumstances honed her tongue and temperament, but the thing I want you to take away from her is that we often don't know what lies underneath the many layers of the people we meet. We judge unfairly sometimes without knowing the whys.

EVADING

Everyone has a story and sometimes it's not one you want to hear, but one they lived through anyway. Be kind.

Thanks to my beta's for this book: Tara, Carrie, Beth, and, of course, my hubs for helping me keep facts straight and getting into the guts of this couple. Your input is invaluable!

Immeasurable thank-yous to the bloggers, fans, and authors who share, like, pimp, and support me and my stories.

Thanks to the team of people I have behind me who make me look good because God knows I could NOT do this all by myself. No one publishes a book—a good one at least—on their own.

Nikki...thank you for smoothing my manuscript to remove my wordiness and horrendous use of punctuation, especially commas!

Heather Lynne...I don't know how I got so lucky to have you in my inner circle and, more importantly, to call you a friend. I love everything about your crazy foul mouth, messy to-do lists, sex-toy reviews, colorful hair, and, of course, that sexy-as-sin voice that will now be put to better use than reading depositions. ;)

Last but not least, thanks to my husband of almost twenty-nine years for being my CFO, my promotions and distributions manager, my research analyst, and whatever else I ask you to help with. Hand to God...there would be no swag without you. I'm slowly but surely letting some of these pieces go so I can focus my efforts on getting all this stuff running around my head down on paper. I love you for your infinite support more than you'll ever understand!

Thank you for taking this journey with me, for buying my book, and for supporting an author you love. Whether that's me or not, your support of your favorite authors cannot be overstated.

If you like this book, *please* tell your friends, your neighbors and shout it from the rooftops. Hell, tell people you don't even like! The best thing you can do to support an author you love is word of mouth and LEAVE A REVIEW on Goodreads or wherever. Even one or two sentences or simply rating the book is helpful for other readers. Reviews are critical to getting a book exposure.

ABOUT THE AUTHOR

This is the hardest part...talking about myself.

I'm just a regular ol' Midwest girl who likes *Game of Thrones* and is obsessed with *Modern Family* and *The Goldbergs*. I run, I eat, I run, I eat. It's a vicious cycle. I love carbs, but there's a love-hate relationship with my ass and thighs. Mostly hate. I like a good cocktail (oh hell...who am I kidding? I love *any* cocktail). I'm a huge creature of habit, but I'll tell you I'm flexible. I read every single day and if I don't get a chance...watch the hell out, I'm a raving bitch. My iPad and I: BFFs. I'm direct and I make no apologies for it. I swear too much. I love alternative music and in my next life, I want to be a badass female rocker. I hate, hate, hate spiders, telemarketers, liver, acne, winter, and loose hairs that fall down my shirt (don't ask, it's a thing).

I have a great job (no...truly it is) outside of writing. My kids and my husband are my entire world and I'd never have made it this far without them. My soul mate husband of over twenty-eight years provides unwavering support and my two grown children know the types of books I write and they don't judge their mom anyway (and my daughter is a beta reader even...yes, that can be awkward...very).

I'm *sincerely* humbled by each and every like on my Facebook page or sign up for my newsletter or outreach from someone who has read and loved my books. I still can't get over the great support. The romance book community is a wonderful and supportive one. I've made more friends since I started this journey than I've made in my life and I'm a pretty affable person. It's surreal. I'm pretty sure it always will be.

In short, I am blessed...and I know it.

If you're a stalker, the first step is to admit it. After that, you can find me in a lot of places, all of which I use with irregular frequency.

In this day and age, with so many great authors and so many new releases, it's challenging to keep up with it all, so if you don't want to miss when my next book is releasing, sign up for my newsletter found on my website. Promise no spamming and you'll only get it when I have something important to say. I also have monthly drawings for free books, gift cards, and even ARCs of my upcoming releases.

Facebook: https://www.facebook.com/pages/KL-Kreig/808927362462053?ref=hl

Kreig's Babes private fan FB page: https://www.facebook.com/groups/646655825434751/

Website: http://klkreig.com

Instagram: klkreig

Goodreads: https://www.goodreads.com/author/show/9845429.K_L_Kreig

Twitter: https://twitter.com/klkreig

TSU: http://www.tsu.co/klkreig

E-mail: klkreig@gmail.com

Made in the USA
Las Vegas, NV
17 January 2022

41658501R00132